POWER OF LOVE

**Unforgettable Stories
that Enrich and Inspire**

T0096146

POWER OF LOVE

Unforgettable Stories that Enrich and Inspire

Athanasius Yohan I

Foreword by
Dr Shashi Tharoor

PENGUIN ENTERPRISE

An imprint of Penguin Random House

PENGUIN ENTERPRISE

USA | Canada | UK | Ireland | Australia
New Zealand | India | South Africa | China

Penguin Enterprise is part of the Penguin Random House group of companies
whose addresses can be found at global.penguinrandomhouse.com

Published by Penguin Random House India Pvt. Ltd
4th Floor, Capital Tower 1, MG Road,
Gurugram 122 002, Haryana, India

First published in Penguin Enterprise by Penguin Random House India 2021

ISBN 9780670095438

Typeset in Adobe Caslon Pro
Printed at Thomson Press India Ltd, New Delhi

www.penguin.co.in

Contents

Foreword   ix

Before You Read   xi

1. The Shocking Underbelly of Metro Cities   1
2. Mahatma Gandhi Looked at Me and Smiled   7
3. Before the Flight Departed   13
4. The Stories Behind the Letters   19
5. The Lotus Eaters   26
6. Illuminating Wayside Scenes   32
7. Waiting for a Good Word   39
8. The Sins of the Saint   46
9. An Elixir for Freedom   52
10. The Beauty of Ugliness   62
11. Memories of My Village   69
12. Being Faithful in Little Things: Living for Others   76

13. Denying Them a Chance to Live   83

14. A Dad for Two Rupees   92

15. Be Kind to Animals   97

16. A Mother's Love   105

17. Geriatrics and the New Generation   112

18. Lesson from Dabba   121

19. What You Are: Appearance and Reality   129

20. Choose for Yourself: Positive Thinking   134

21. I Hate My Husband!   141

22. In Search of Faithfulness   148

23. Keep This Secret   156

24. Worthy of Love: The Way to Work   161

25. The Gains behind the Pains   170

26. The Human Touch: A Smile Also Matters   177

27. Gratitude   185

28. The Tomb with the Light of Faithfulness   190

29. Mend Your Mind to Make Your Life   195

30. A True Friend   200

31. What You Can't Buy with Money   206

32. Where the Freedom of Mind Begins   215

33. The Incarnations of Mercy   221

34. When the Doctor Falls Sick   227

35. Compassion   237

36. A Starless Night   244

37. Contentment 249
38. Symbol of Love 254
39. Stolen Childhood 262

Notes 271
Acknowledgment 279
About the Author 281

Foreword

In today's increasingly stratified, divided and uncertain world, we are susceptible to viewing our fellow human beings with hostility and suspicion. We are vulnerable to forgetting how much more unites us than divides us, no matter how different we may be from each other.

In this introspective book, Athanasius Yohan I, the Metropolitan of the Believers Eastern Church, has examined with great detail the questions that plague us all, questions which we often seek to avoid: Are we living a just life? Is that even possible? Through a series of revealing stories, he discusses his own struggles with these difficult dilemmas, and through them provides guidance on how to live a good life.

From childhood lessons on the importance of honesty to the humble backgrounds of history's great writers, he finds inspiration in many areas. His approach to life is worthy of praise, and reminds us of one of the book's most important lessons: To be aware of the great beauty and compassion around us, and to not give in to the despair that too often acts as a temptation. A moving guide on living with honesty and goodness, I commend the distinguished Metropolitan for bringing to us the *Power of Love*—a most timely guide for navigating these exceptional times.

Dr Shashi Tharoor
Member of Parliament (Lok Sabha), India
Chairman, Information Technology
Committee of Parliament

Before You Read

The Father of our beloved Bharat is Mahatma Gandhi. He loved people more than himself, especially the poor and downtrodden. He once said, 'He who spins before the poor, inviting them to do likewise, serves God as no one else does.'[1] Kindness and compassion marked his life. St Teresa of Calcutta (Mother Teresa) said, 'As far as I am concerned, the greatest suffering in the world is feel alone, unwanted and unloved.'[2] Sounds like a real mother talking. Strange, but true! When Mother Teresa died, it was said, 'The Mother of India died.'

Life void of love, warmth, feelings is the nature of 'hell'. The image comes to mind of many, of hell is blazing fire, pitch dark, utter darkness and torment.

It is said that the historian and philosopher Voltaire, hallucinating on his death bed cried out, 'I am in flames.'[3]

Dante's Inferno[4] describes the deepest, hardest bottom of hell is a silent, icy place. The worst of sinners, the most evil are immersed in an eternally frozen polluted dark swamp. These worst of sinners, their sins were of hate, betrayal, feelingless, cruelty, void of kindness—and now their punishment is to be condemned in the bottom of hell where there is no feelings of love, but frightening silence and all alone without compassion.

Think about it. No wonder, there are people that say about themselves that they are living in hell. Yes, they may be physically living in a mansion with all the luxury and power, yet their soul is, as Mother Teresa said, in great suffering, void of love and passion.

Love is the only remedy that can cure all evils in our world.

Our hearts long and hunger for love, without it, we die on the inside. How many a family, people exist as living dead beings—for the lack of kindness and love!

The most powerful weapon in the universe is love and my hope is, these real life stories and words you read in this book will bring transformation and hope for you, my reader, and through you many others will find love and hope. And no more, you or anyone else needs to live in hell, without it.

You and I can make the difference. And we must.

Famous psychologist, Dr Harry F. Harlow conducted one of the most amazing, history changing experiment at his university of Wisconsin Laboratory in 1950.[5]

His attempt was to prove that the nature of love is embodied and formed between infants and mothers, first it was through primarily emotional rather than psychological.

Secondly, this emotional development was only possible through physical closeness such as constant loving embrace, affirming eye contact, emotional warmth. His experiment gives us a window to understand the desperate need for love and how it works.

This is how his experiment went.

He separated infant monkeys from their mothers a few hours after birth, then arranged for the young animals to be 'raised' by two kinds of surrogate monkey mother machines, both equipped to dispense milk. One mother was made out of bare wire mesh. The other was a wire mother covered with soft terry cloth. Harlow's first observation was that monkeys who had a choice of mothers spent far more time clinging to the terry cloth surrogates, even when their physical nourishment came from bottles mounted on the bare wire mothers. This suggested that infant love was no simple response to the satisfaction of physiological needs. Attachment was not primarily about hunger or thirst. It could not be reduced to nursing.

Then Harlow modified his experiment and made a second important observation. When he separated the infants into two groups and gave them no choice between two types of mothers, all the monkeys drank equal amounts and grew physically at the same rate. But the similarities ended there. Monkeys who had soft, tactile contact with their terry cloth mothers behave quite differently than monkeys whose mothers were made out of cold, hard wire. Harlow hypothesized that members of the first group benefited from a psychological resource—emotional attachment—unavailable to members of the second. By providing reassurance and security to infants, cuddling kept normal development on track.

What exactly did Harlow see that convinced him emotional attachment made a decisive developmental difference? When the experimental subjects were frightened by strange, loud objects, such as teddy bears beating drums, monkeys raised by terry cloth surrogates made bodily contact with their mothers, rubbed against them, and eventually calmed down. Harlow theorized that they used their mothers as a 'psychological base of operations,' allowing them to remain playful and inquisitive after the initial fright had subsided. In contrast, monkeys raised by wire mesh surrogates did not retreat to their mothers when scared. Instead, they threw themselves on the floor, clutched themselves, rocked back and forth, and screamed in terror. These activities closely resembled the behaviours of autistic and deprived children frequently observed in institutions as well as the pathological behaviour of adults confined to mental institutions. Harlow noted. The awesome power of attachment and loss over mental health and illness could hardly have been performed more dramatically.

This proves that mammals—we humans—do not live by material things, right and wrong, facts and figures, harsh, lifeless behaviour and response—but our hearts long for soft, kind, understanding and loving embrace and response.

Our world is dying without the oxygen of love and kindness. There are nations that spend far more on creating weapons of destruction than for food and clothing for the suffering millions!

Where is this hate and war come from? What can we do about it? Mother Teresa often said, 'Love begins in your home.'[6]

My hope and prayer to Almighty is that we will forget caste, creed, religion, nationality, colour, rich or poor—and we see others with a little more kindliness and affection.

Best wishes to you as you journey with me through these pages.

1

The Shocking Underbelly of Metro Cities

One morning some years ago, I reached Mumbai for a meeting. I opened the windows of the hotel room where I was staying. A cold-winged light breeze descended into the room. Mumbai city was waking up. No, I recalled: cities never sleep. Towering skyscrapers of the metropolis and concrete structures caressing the cloud! Lengthy roads stretching between them like long dark veins! It was amusing to see vehicles moving in orderly rows.

The calling bell rang, breaking the train of my thoughts. I opened the door. A boy stood there, holding out a newspaper. Dressed in a long pair of trousers and a cotton vest, he wore a rather grim look on his face. I bought a newspaper. He moved on to the next room, still without a smile on his face. They were English newspapers. Good hotels generally supply three or four newspapers to their guests.

Leaving the newspapers on the teapoy, I prepared a cup of black tea. The porch of the hotel room had a chair. Sitting there, one could enjoy the beauty of the metropolis. Sipping the black tea, I opened the newspaper. Usually, on busy days, my newspaper reading would be restricted to a quick scan of the headlines. That day was no different.

I ran through the front page of the newspaper. Suddenly, a news photograph caught my eyes. It showed a human child sucking milk from the udder of a street dog. I looked at the photo once more. Yes, indeed! It was a human child. I could not believe my eyes. An eerie numbness crept all over my body and my heart began to pound. My eyes fell on the caption: 'This Dog is my mother!'

There are some lives like this amidst the city's pockets of prosperity. A Mr Sharma who worked in the social service organization I was part of, was with me then.

Quickly I called him. 'Look, Mr Sharma. Did you see this unbelievable piece of news?' Sharma came and asked anxiously, 'What happened?' I showed him the news story.

'This is a normal sight in this city,' said Sharma. 'Mumbai is not what it appears to be. It has a large world of poverty and deprivation behind it.' Sharma began to speak about the city's orphans and their pains . . . It was true, and I was no less aware of these. Nonetheless, how pathetic the image of a hungry human child suckling on the udder of a street dog was!

Even as I was returning home from the trip, that image remained etched in my mind as a rankling twinge of pain.

Tired millions sleep in the by-lanes of poverty in the world of wealth. Those without even a one-room house, who cannot afford a full meal a day, who have never known their parents, who sacrifice their lives on red streets, who are bound to the stench of the slums, who sleep by the wayside and merge into the busy city life even before the city wakes up. My heart ached as I thought that my country was no less theirs too.

This was not the India that Shri Vinoba Bhave, Mahatma Gandhi, Dr Ambedkar and Swami Vivekananda had dreamed of. The majority here are denied opportunities. Hundreds of thousands of children wander in the streets of Mumbai and Kolkata. Drug Mafia ensnares the children who come running away from their homes. In fact, it is not sympathy, but action plans that are required to uplift them.

A few months later, I went to Mumbai again to address a meeting. In the evening, I stepped out into the street. Some children with outstretched arms surrounded me as I was waiting for the signal to cross the road. I had had several such experiences. Suddenly, I became annoyed. Obviously, they were sent by some business lobby of money-making schemers, I thought to myself.

'I won't give them a single paisa,' I told myself. There were many others begging in the street. Mothers were stretching forth their arms for coins, carrying frail, hungry and naked babies. I didn't like seeing such sights.

Suddenly, there was a sound from behind me. It seemed to be piercing right into me. 'Sir, my father died of TB. Mother is too sick to beg. I have three hungry siblings crying for food. Give me something, please.' The signal turned green. Now was the time for me to walk across the road. But I could not move. I was dumbfounded and immobilised. The signal switched to red again.

I turned around and looked at her face. She stood there with outstretched arms. She was hardly nine years old. She had thick black hair, was so long that almost fell below her knees. Beads of sweat and dust were visible across her face, marked with distinct channels of dried sweat. 'Had she been born in a rich man's family, she would have easily won the world beauty pageant,' I thought. She had such extraordinary beauty and large black eyes.

Her torn, patched clothes and soiled black feet could not conceal her beauty. Her beautiful shining face smeared in dust, and brightly gleaming skin reminded me of the people of Kashmir where I had lived years ago. Her eyes reflected flashes of hunger. I gave her some money, much more than what she had expected. Her eyes conveyed her gratitude. As I walked away, another child filled my memory. I felt as though a stranger was walking along with me.

A question arose in my mind. Or perhaps it was a question the invisible messenger was asking me, 'What do you think of that beggar girl?'

Then, the image of another girl appeared in my mind. I did not know the name of the girl who had asked me for alms. But I knew the name of the other girl. She had her parents and her own room in her own house. She had everything she needed. That was a beautiful young girl from a family I knew well.

'So, what's the value of that beggar girl?' the invisible mystic asked. 'I think her value is equal to that of the value of my life.' I respond in silence.

I kept walking. Now, he was not with me; that young street girl was also not with me. But, where did he go? Who was that stranger?

Was he my guardian angel? Or was he the guardian angel of that street girl? It was not the time to think and find an answer. It was the moment of a turning point in my life.

That day, as I was boarding the flight home after my assignments, the face of that street girl also stayed in a corner of my mind.

It did not take much longer to happen. I had already decided to do something for orphan children. I drew up a project to educate the children deprived of opportunities and lacking in avenues and resources. By the grace of God, we as of date were now able to educate and care for about 130,000 children in various countries.

Some sights and encounters are like that. They turn out to be the spring-board to new beginnings. Those poignant sights were the beginning of our child welfare project called 'Hope For Children.'[1]

Why did Mahatma Gandhi live as a fakir? He had understood the piteous plight of the village folks. When a child asked him, 'Why don't you wear a shirt?' he answered, 'I need 400 million shirts.'[2] The population of India then was 400 million. He could not turn a blind eye to those who had nothing themselves.

The great souls in history dreamed of a welfare state. The Buddha, who said that desire was the root cause of all suffering,[3] Karl Marx who visualized a world of socialist equality,[4] and Lord Jesus who preached about the peaceful Kingdom of God—all of them desired the welfare of humankind.[5] 'Do not inure any being either strong or weak, in the world. All beings tremble before violence. All fear death. All love life. See yourself in others. Then whom can you hurt? What harm can you do?' said Buddha.[6]

We don't require grand projects to love and help others. The needy are all around us—those who are hungry, or without money for treatment, without money to buy books and a school-bag when the school opens, without the means for food . . . and so on. We must reserve a small drop of tear for them. We must give them a little touch of love. That is how humanness can bear fruit.

The poor and broken you help could be God appearing before you in disguise. Mother Teresa said, 'If you can't feed a hundred people, then feed just one.'[7]

2

Mahatma Gandhi
Looked at Me and Smiled

My primary schooling was at a Government School which lies nestled in the heart of Kuttanad in the South Indian state of Kerala. We passed through the idyllic sights of Kuttanad as we ambled to school every day. The place was an open textbook of local wisdom imparting lessons of goodness. The cranes and white pigeons idling in the paddy fields would get a little annoyed and fly away as we got closer to them. Soon, they would again descend on the field and the ridges.

During my school days, letters delivered at home carried stamps with the pictures of Mahatma Gandhi, Jawaharlal Nehru, the Taj Mahal, etc., on them. The shrewd ones among us would do a clever thing. If the stamps didn't carry the impression of the postal seal, we would get them carefully removed after soaking them in water. Then we pasted them on new letters before posting. The stamps were only worth five, ten or twenty-five paisa. Still, we had a champion-like feeling of elation after using those cleverly collected stamps. Our faces would beam with the jubilation of having outsmarted someone.

Many children do that. I too have done that many a time.

Years later, (This happened during the early 1970s) I got the opportunity to travel across India and abroad as a speaker and a trainer. Once, I was invited to a venue in Delhi to give lectures on the topic of honesty or integrity. I started preparing notes for it by referring to many books and Holy Scriptures.

Suddenly, a question came to my mind, 'Have you been honest in everything?'

I ignored the question. 'After all, do all teachers meticulously follow what they teach? Who doesn't have shortcomings?' I tried to reason with myself.

Those childhood stamps suddenly popped up before me. Taj Mahal, Gandhi and Nehru stood before me. They were smiling. I understood the meaning of that smile. They seemed to be asking questions like 'Weren't you cheating by reusing the canceled stamps? You stole the money that should have gone to the government, didn't you? How can the government get money to function if you don't pay for the stamp?'

Before going to speak in that seminar that day, I did something. I went straight to the post office and bought stamps worth a considerable amount of money. I went to the Post Master and told him about what I had done during my childhood. Then I tore up all the stamps and dumped it in the trash bin that I just purchased from the post office. It was a deeply humble honest thing to do. It was important to my conscience to make the confession to the postmaster and destroy the stamps as he witnessed my remorse.

The postmaster looked at me in wonder. He must have thought I was crazy. 'I don't have any mental problems. I have to do this so that I can teach others about honesty,' I told him.

'Khuda aap ko barkat de betta (God bless you, son),' the stocky old postmaster said, nodding his head.

From that day, I had a rare sense of self-confidence when I spoke before an audience. The gratification of being a 'true winner' was a very special feeling. It was quite unlike the false jubilation of the childhood 'fake winner.'

Perhaps, there was a special reason for me to do so. My father was known for his honesty in our village. This is not merely what I say. Everyone in our locality acknowledges it.

Once, I was returning from school with dozens of other students, a twenty-five paisa coin fell off from someone's pocket who was walking ahead of me. Making sure that no one noticed it, I took the coin and slipped it into my pocket. I was home, elated with the treasure I had chanced upon.

At home, I told my father about the coin I found on the street.

'Is it yours?' my father asked.

'No,' I said.

'Then it belongs to someone who lost it. You must find that person and return it.'

'But, how can I find that person? Hundreds of people walk along this way every day,' I responded with a little sadness.

'You must ask your school friends—whether they lost their money, where do they think they have lost it, and so on. Do that for the next thirty days. Then, if nobody claims it, you may take it and buy sweets,' my father replied.

I agreed. For the next month, I carried the coin looking for the person who had lost it. I really had no idea who he or she was.

After a month, my father took up the case for hearing. 'I couldn't find the owner of this coin,' I made my plea.

My father pronounced his final judgement. 'Then, you may buy sweets with this.'

On the following day I did so. Although it was a trifle, its seriousness was significant, and so was the outcome.

The lessons in honesty and faithfulness my father gave me have remained to this day as indelible pictures of virtue etched in my mind.

If we do not correct the smallest of our mistakes, it can lead us to big trouble. The people who remain steadfast in honesty and integrity will succeed in life and also earn respect.

Once, a man came to see me. After talking to him for a while, I asked, 'What do you do?' He replied that he was a firewood vendor. I asked him whether he bought logs, broke those into pieces and sold it as firewood in the market. He said that he was a wholesaler dealing in truckloads of firewood.

I asked him if he did not have to tell a few lies as part of this business. 'Can anyone do this business otherwise?' he grinned.

'Aren't you a God-fearing man? How can you engage in a business which makes you lie?' I continued. His reply made me laugh.

'Because telling lies is necessary in this line of business, I merely pack the logs and give it to someone else. It is he who goes to the market and sells,' he said.

It is a routine business and even a religious devotee thinks that he cannot run his business without lying. It is incorrect to say that one has to lie in order to do business. But one may have to pay a price in order to remain honest.

I remember hearing the story of a renowned US senator.[1] Wherever he went, people asked him, 'How come you are so different from most politicians? Why do you give such a high priority to a principled life?' In reply, he recounted an experience he had had as a small boy when he and his father went fishing in a lake one morning, carrying their fishing rod and bait.

Their fishing licenses stated that they could carry home only the fish they caught after noon. (In the United States, license is required to fish in lakes.)

They waited for long for fishes to bite the bait. Suddenly, the boy felt a tug on his fishing rod. 'Daddy, Daddy, fish!' he called out loudly. Father helped him to reel in the fishing line and pull the fish off the water. A stunningly big fish hung at the end of the fishing line.

'Look Daddy, I've caught a big fish,' the boy shouted excitedly. 'Daddy, we can cook it. Mom will be delighted.'

But his father said, 'So my son, it's five minutes to noon. The law allows us to carry home only the fish we catch after noon. Unfortunately, it's not 12.00 p.m. yet.'

'But Daddy, there's no one here. We are all alone in this lake. No one will get to know of it.'

But his father was firm, 'Son, there are still five minutes to twelve. It's not yet 12.00 p.m.'

'Oh, Daddy, it's a matter of five minutes only,' the boy began to sob and plead.

'My son, maybe only five minutes remain. But . . . no . . . we cannot take this fish home,' he said, throwing the fish back into the lake.

It might look like an insignificant matter. But nonetheless, his father's commitment to honesty left such a profound impact on him as to help him become a successful politician later in life. It made him remain committed to doing the right thing, whether anyone saw it or not, whether anyone knew about it or not, and regardless of the cost he had to pay for it.

Our true self is what we live when no one sees us. The lines of the great poet Ulloor S. Parameswara Iyer are very pertinent: 'For the one who carries a lamp, the entire world turns bright.'[2]

Be honest in all that you think, say and do, like karma it will come back to you in the long run, hundredfold.

3

Before the Flight Departed

In Syrian Christian homes, the eldest son becomes the patriarchal authority after the death of the parents. The matriarchal system of inheritance is still prevalent among a few Hindu families. When the joint family system was followed in some areas, it was the uncle who became the patriarch. At our home, my eldest brother became the household chieftain after the death of my father. All of us brothers obeyed him as we had been obeying our father.

I went abroad for studies, and when my field of work expanded to include South East Asia, Europe and North America, I used to return to visit my home from time to time. After the visit, when I took leave, my eldest brother saw me off with prayers. I always set off on my journey with the blessings of my eldest brother who had inherited the mantle of paternal authority.

Once, on the eve of my departure, we had some difference of opinion over a couple of issues. We argued with each other, although it was not quite a quarrel. Everyone does have a few occasions like this when we cannot agree with the ideas of those who are dear to us. I felt very bad. Dark clouds gathered into my mind, making my heart heavy.

After a few winks of sleep somehow, I got up early in the morning and dressed up. My only thought was to reach Cochin airport, board the flight to Mumbai and catch the LH Flight to Germany that night itself. I talked to everyone except my eldest brother. He was sitting right there on a chair on the porch.

It was very foggy outside. The day was just breaking. Even after the early morning bath, it remained humid. The car taking me to the airport was already standing by. I picked up my bag and another suitcase and walked towards the car. 'Bye, bye,' I said as if to everyone and waved my hands. I got into the car. Slowly, the car wheeled away. It picked up speed as soon as it crossed our courtyard and hit the road. The distance from home kept increasing as the car accelerated.

By now the daylight was visible. The road was empty. Suddenly someone seemed to be whispering from within me: 'You are being arrogant. You are going away without the prayer and blessing from your brother.' I realized that it was true. But I had already started my journey. 'Well, after all, it's only a trivial thing,' I reasoned with myself, finding a justification. However, my mind was troubled.

Suddenly, I told the driver, 'Please stop the car.'

'Oh! Have you forgotten anything, Sir?' he asked.

'No. Turn around and go back home,' I said.

'It's already late now. Shouldn't we reach the airport in time?' he parried, being hesitant.

'It's okay,' I said, 'I can catch the next flight if I miss this one. But this matter is not like that. It's something I can't afford to miss. We will return quickly after reaching home.'

The driver did not know what was going on. Well, he need not know either. He turned the vehicle around. Our village folks consider it inauspicious to be called from behind, to turn back, or to have a cat cross your path once you have started a journey. It has been an unwritten rule that one should never do that. Probably, the driver was thinking along these lines, as his worried face seemed to suggest. However, he drove fast and reached home. He stopped the car in front of our house.

Sitting in the car, I glanced at the house. I could hardly believe my eyes. My eldest brother was still there, sitting on the chair on the porch.

I stepped out of the car and briskly walked towards him. He looked at me emotionally.

I bent down and touched his feet. 'Achaya (a term for one's eldest brother), please forgive me. Pray over me and send me off with your blessings,' I said.

Tears welled up in our eyes. Rising from the chair, he said, 'I knew you would come back.' My eyes began to fill. I felt a couple of teardrops falling onto my cheeks. The dark clouds that had gathered in my mind were turning into showers.

Placing his hands on my shoulders, he prayed for my journey. He embraced me affectionately after the prayer. Patting me on the back, he said, 'Go and return safely. May God bless you.'

Oh! He was waiting there to say this. By then, everyone at home had gathered there. When I got into the car, my eldest brother waved his hands. All the faces bore smiles radiating sheer joy. The risen sun stood above the fields, as a witness to everything. Light had now fallen all around, making everything bright. The car sped ahead. It moved faster, perhaps as I had become lighter.

For our lives to be blessed and prosperous, whether at home or in society, it is essential that we respect our elders and those in authority.

There is a bit of history behind my seeking the blessings of my eldest brother.

When I was a child, my mother came to me one fine morning and said, 'Today, you are going to the nursery.' She held my hand and led me to my father who was sitting on a chair and said, 'Son, touch your father's feet and take his blessings.' I touched his feet in obeisance. He laid his hands on my head, saying: 'God bless you, my son.' Those were all the words he uttered. But they still keep ringing in my ears and mind.

When I went to school for the first time, my mother asked me to touch the feet of my guru and take his blessings. I did so.

It was my mother who trained me to treat my teachers and elders with respect and reverence.

Years passed by. I completed my school in India and College in the USA and my responsibilities made me a kind of world traveler. Once in a while, I returned to my homeland for the work I did and became successful in life.

One of those times on my return to India, I went to my little village Niranam to visit my relatives. I walked past the house where I had grown up as a child and reached a familiar bridge. Then, I saw my Guru that taught me in the Kindergarten, coming in the opposite direction.

He must be quite old, really old now. He was wearing only a mundu (a single-piece, white linen cloth) and no shirt. As I had changed a lot, I thought that probably he would not recognize me.

We came face to face on the bridge. 'Sir,' I called. 'Kutti (young child) . . .' he replied.

One of my fondest memories overwhelmed me. I bent down and touched the feet of my old teacher. Here was a frail old man advanced in age and infirmity. My teacher! I recall him repeating the words, 'God bless you.' I can never forget that meeting.

He was my teacher. We called him Kaniyan Asan (master). In fact, we were afraid to go to Kaniyan Asan's nursery. We had to be lured with sweets to go to this local nursery known as kalari. As my first guru, he took my little fingers and made me write the Malayalam alphabets 'A, Aa, E, Ee . . .' upon sand, and taught me to pronounce them after him.

By the time I woke up from the reverie, the car was already at the airport. I didn't miss the flight.

I am proud of being an Indian for a million reasons. One of the most precious things about our Indian culture is respecting and honouring our elders. May God protect our culture.

Cherish respect.

4

The Stories Behind the Letters

Of all the books I have read, it is the life story of a young man that has inspired me most. It happened some years ago. This young man lived in London. The pomp and pleasures of the city of London were beyond his reach. Still, his mind was full of dreams and aspirations.

There are so many variations of the stories about the early years of his life. But all agree on the main events that shaped his life.

He dreamed of becoming a great writer. But he did not have the wherewithal or circumstances to nurture such a dream.

He was the second of eight children to his parents. His father, who had a difficult time managing money and was constantly in debt, was imprisoned. Due to his family's unsteady situation, his schooling got interrupted and unimpressive, leaving him always anxious about his future.

He was sent to work in a factory where he slogged in the unclean environment and laboured ten hours, six days a week if only to satisfy his hunger and to take care of his family.

Despite intense fatigue and lack of adequate rest, he continued to cherish his dreams. From his young age, he had an astonishing capacity for concentration and focus which was vivid in his habit of reading. He did not give it up, as he went on with his career in Law Office and then as a Newspaper Reporter.

By the age of twenty-one, he began to contribute short stories and essays to periodicals. His career as a writer of fiction began with a sketch that he deposited anonymously with fear and trembling, in the mailbox of the *Monthly Magazine* as 'A Dinner at Poplar Walk'. Finally, when he saw it in print at a newsstand, he could not believe his eyes. 'My eyes were so dimmed with joy and pride that they could not bear the street and were not fit to be seen there,' later he recalled. Tears welled up in his eyes and he sought a place to weep. Waves of sheer joy surged within him and he soon wrote another eight 'sketches,' all anonymous, until that published in August 1834.

At twenty-two, he was hired by the Morning Chronicle, a distinguished paper. There, his editor not only paid him for the sketches but encouraged him saying, 'You should keep writing even if that meant less reporting.'[1]

This young man came to be known as the world-renowned novelist, Charles Dickens (1812-1870). A few words of encouragement and affirmation strengthened his heart to climb the heights that he would have given up. That became oxygen for his soul. The impoverished casual labourer became a world-famous writer.

The lives of Abraham Lincoln, Napoleon, Martin Luther King, Mahatma Gandhi, Beethoven, Tolstoy and Dostoevsky were not different either. They never gave up on their dreams when faced with impediments. The few good words they received became their window to the limitless sky of possibilities. The world needed them. Charles Dickens's experience has inspired me too. While it was in high school, I first read Charles Dickens's book, *David Copperfield* and I still love it. His other timeless classic is *A Christmas Carol*.

How immense was the power of the encouragement Dickens received! A small inspiring word can fashion great people out of ordinary ones.

I look back at my own life at this juncture. I too have received a few goodness-filled letters—some inspiring words that invigorated me to go ahead.

A few years after my high school life, I received an inland letter. Written in an excellent hand, it carried the inscription 'Ayyappan' outside it. Who could be this Ayyappan writing to me, I wondered. But my eyes flooded when I opened the letter and read it!

This Ayyappan sir was my teacher who had taught me in the high school years. He somehow managed to find out my address and wrote to me.

He reminded me of what I had forgotten. How I had visited his house to learn thoroughly even as my friends were busy playing, how I begged for his forgiveness whenever I did something wrong, confessing that, 'I was at fault, please forgive me.' The letter also carried his blessing, 'May God bless you, my student.'

It strengthened me a lot. I was overjoyed when I realized that there was someone—none other than my teacher—who remembered me and spoke well of me. I think it is a common feeling with everyone.

My teacher Ayyappan's letter multiplied my self-confidence. It immensely contributed to the formation of my personality and dreams.

It was a momentous event that led me to my goal. That event convinced me that the world needed me.

I have been doing a radio talk programme in my mother tongue Malayalam for three and a half decades in the state of Kerala in India. Every household in Kerala had a radio in the 1980s. In Indian villages, radio was the popular medium of entertainment until the television arrived. It was through the radio that an entire generation appreciated news, movie songs, plays, and speeches.

When I returned to Kerala towards the end of 1984, a friend of mine asked me to start a radio programme. He thought it would do much good. Those were the early days of my social service career. That was also the time when our voluntary organization had initiated its socio-developmental works and awareness programmes. As it was the golden age of radio, my friends suggested that it would be immensely beneficial if a series of lectures could be given addressing a family crisis, alcoholism, etc., apart from a few music programmes. As I was trained in mass media and communication I was pretty good at it.

However, my main concern was whether my Malayalam was good enough to give lectures on radio. After all, I had been in North India after high school, and eight years later I moved to America and Europe. One should not break out into English or Hindi while speaking in Malayalam on the radio.

'I don't think I can do it,' I told my friend. 'First of all, I have a language issue. Secondly, I'm afraid I don't have the time.'

My friend said, 'God will help you, and I believe in you. You can do it. Don't give it up. You are trained for it and people need you.'

Finally, I decided to prepare a fifty-day radio programme. We started recording it in the studio and then launched the broadcast.

I had to reach the studio for recording very early in the morning. It was a daily fifteen-minute programme. I was presenting the programme in simple, conversational language. Something amazing happened. Those who listened to the programme began to write letters. Not one or two, but thousands. We even got up to 8,000 letters a day. We had to put volunteers to manage those letters and make special arrangements to reply to them.

A few words of encouragement from my friends had made it a hugely successful programme.

I was startled by the letters that kept pouring into the office. Most of them sought advice regarding family crises, alcoholic issues, suicidal tendencies, apprehensions about the future, and so on. The majority of those letters asked for some sort of guidance. There were also a few letters which were critical of the programme. But those letters were virtual windows giving a realistic view of society. Like the observation by a Malayalam poet that the real world is not the romantic picture we see, those letters made me realize that what we saw outwardly was not the actual life of the people of Kerala.

My heart ached. I also felt their pain. I felt that I must speak to them again as they were waiting for my words. They needed me. Those talks transformed the lives of many people. For three decades the radio programme called 'Athmeeya Yathra' (Spiritual Journey) continued. As I look back, it becomes clear that the words of encouragement and those letters of support actually made it possible.

An independent media survey reported that every day nearly sixty per cent of Kerala households tuned into the radio programme at 6.15 a.m. The programme would start with an introduction statement on the theme of that day's talk and end the lead statement . . . 'I am K. P. Yohannan (my birth name before I became the Episcopa and the Metropolitan, adopting a new name) and this is Athmeeya Yathra.' Like the lyrics of a folk song, it became ingrained in the Malayali mind. Its local style of presentation became extremely popular. Even as the introductory music played, children from some houses would shout, 'I am

K.P. Yohannan and this is Spiritual Journey.' Mothers would giggle listening to them. Households of my audience would consider me as a family member. Such acceptability was the highest honour a speaker could ever get.

Most Malayalees I came across in many countries all over the world have told me how they regularly listened to the radio programme 'Spiritual Journey.' They have also narrated its impact and the difference it made in their lives.

Words of motivation and encouragement have inestimable potential. If possible, try practicing to say a few words of inspiration and encouragement at least to a few people every day. You can begin this good habit by telling a few encouraging words to your wife, your husband, your parents, your children, your colleagues, and to your friends.

Say to someone today, 'I am so proud of you. You are very special and the world needs you.'

5

The Lotus Eaters

Knock, knock . . . Someone was knocking at the door. I was getting ready to go to office in the morning. In my village, if someone knocks at the door so early in the morning, it must be some emergency.

'Who is knocking at the door? Did something unfortunate happen to anyone in the morning?' I wondered as I opened the door without even finishing buttoning up my shirt. A young man stood there. It seemed to me that I had come across him a couple of times earlier. He had a feigned smile on his face.

'Yes, what's the matter?' I asked.

'Oh. Nothing special. I just came over, that's all.' He replied with a sly expression.

It is usual for some people to say 'nothing' if someone enquires about their well-being. It is only a natural reaction.

Even when they have serious matters to convey, they might still say 'nothing' to begin with.

'Still, what's the matter? I asked again. I finished buttoning up the shirt. It was time for me to leave. There was a special meeting that day. I insist on being present at least five minutes before any meeting.

'I need a hundred rupees,' the young man said in a hushed tone.

'For what?'

'It's something urgent.' He did not want to reveal the reason, I reckoned. Or, there could be no reason at all. If he was a helpless beggar I would have given some help without much thinking about it. But, here an able-bodied young man is asking for a specific amount not as a loan either. I asked him, if he has no work to make some money.

'Oh! Where can I get a job now? There's no work.' There was a sense of carelessness in his voice.

'Well, that won't be difficult,' I said, slipping my feet into the shoes lying next to the chair. 'There's enough work here. Let me see if I can help you.'

I went out and called the elderly neighbour living next door. All of us in the neighbourhood called him 'chakkara maman' (his nickname). He was a sprightly middle-aged man, short and rather stocky. An enthusiastic person with salt-and-pepper hair. Everyone liked Chakkara Maman. He had the deftness to handle everything with a sense of humour. He would also give apt advice on difficult issues and help anyone in need. A good and lovable man, overall.

'Chakkara Maman,' I called aloud.

'I'm coming.' He came running, quickly crossing the mud-ridge in the rice field. His regular outfit was a lungi and a sleeveless vest. In case he was travelling somewhere, he would also have a large white shawl upon his shoulders.

'What's the matter, Who is he?' Chakkara Maman asked, carefully observing the young man.

'Uncle, he has no work. We need to help him. Can we give him some work?' I said.

'Oh! Do you know him?'

'No.'

'Then . . .'

'Oh . . . it doesn't matter. He needs some money urgently,' I recommended for him. 'After all, he's a young man. And also very healthy. We may help him if we can. That's all.'

'Where's your house?' Chakkara Maman looked at him closely again.

He answered, again with an artificial smile: 'Beyond the Kattunilam church, across the field of Kunjavarachan.'

'Wait! There's enough work here,' Chakkara Maman said, then went inside and came back with a pickaxe.

'Come on, Boy. You can dig up this land along with me today,' Chakkara Maman looked at him. I nodded my head in agreement.

'It's already time for me to go to the office, uncle,' I said.

'Okay, son. Go ahead. I'll take care of things here.' That was the typical Chakkara Maman, always quick and responsible like a manager.

'Listen! This uncle will give you work for a few days. Now I'm going to the office. When I return in the evening, I'll give you more than the usual wage. Now, follow Chakkara Maman's instructions and do the work he assigns to you. Right?' I told the young man.

He looked into my face and then cast his eyes down. I had made up my mind to give him more than the usual wage anyway. I went inside, combed my hair and went off to Thiruvalla. I had the satisfaction of having been able to help a young man.

When I came back in the evening, I found no one around. There was no sign of any work done. I called Chakkara Maman, 'Chakkara Maman, where is our man?'

Chakkara Maman came hurriedly, beaming with a smile: 'Soon after you left, he absconded from here. He said he didn't want such work. He's quite a shammer.'

I was surprised. He was a smart and healthy young man, but unwilling to work. He wanted easy money.

Later I will learn more about him. He lived in a leaking, thatched house beside the stream beyond Kunjavarachan's paddy field. His wife worked as a domestic help in a couple of houses. He had two daughters—one in grade two and the other was only eighteen months old.

He was the head of a family burdened by starvation and hunger. His wife worked hard to earn their daily bread, but he wouldn't even move a little finger to help her. He would idle away his time by loitering around, smoking and playing rummy.

Doling out money to such indolent people is hazardous. It encourages their indolence and laziness. It is futile to think of supporting them with the offer of some work. These laggards refuse to do work or undertake physical labour.

Ours is a serene and idyllic place. People work hard and are generally enthusiastic to plough, sow, reap and thresh paddy. Kuttanad ranks second in rice production in Kerala. Even when they suffer loss and damage of crops from fallen dykes and devastating gales, they never despair, but spiritedly get back to their fields sowing and cultivating. Pests play havoc before the harvesting season. Sometimes torrential rain breeches the levees surrounding the paddy fields and inundates the fields. Undeterred, they empty the submerged fields and raise their crops afresh with increased vigour.

Many families have prospered through sheer hard work. When I travel along that way today, I can see splendid concrete houses in place of the old thatched huts. Today there are no thatched huts in our area. The village has prospered through hard work and perseverance.

Once someone asked Charles Dickens about the secret of his success. 'Whatever I have tried to do in life, I have tried with all my heart to do it well; whatever I have devoted myself to, I have devoted myself completely; in great aims and in small I have always thoroughly been in earnest,' he answered.[1]

One's approach and attitude to life are very important. As I have learned from classes on personality, our knowledge accounts for only 15 per cent of our success; attitude contributes to the remaining 85 per cent.

Lazy people have a peculiar nature. They always keep blaming those who have succeeded in life and have money and means. They keep on criticizing, 'Oh, see his house . . . He's bought a car . . . Where does he get all the money from?' and so on.

The American poet Henry Longfellow (1807-1882) once wrote, 'Something attempted, something done, Has earned a night's repose'[2] Yes. Great people have achieved success in the quietness of the night.

It is the will to work hard that gift you with success.

6

Illuminating Wayside Scenes

Travel! The preparation and logistics associated with it make me uneasy. But it was essential for me to travel to discharge my responsibilities. Even though sometimes I disliked it, I had to travel.

My travel across India has made me aware of the cultural diversity of our land. It is a land where Kashmiris, Punjabis, Marathis, Gujaratis, Biharis, Odiyas, Bengalis, Tamilians, Malayalees and all others live together by preserving and celebrating the colourful umbrella of our distinctiveness. It was during my travels that I had close encounters with the beauty of diversification.

One gets different kinds of experiences while travelling in countries such as the United States, the United Kingdom, Germany, Iceland, Mexico, Nepal, Myanmar, Korea, South Africa, etc. People are alike in spite of their cultural differences. I have come across people who faithfully discharge responsibilities in many places. I have also seen absolutely irresponsible people, as well. It is the sense of responsibility that teaches one to remain active in life.

Travels are my textbooks. The people we come across, the sights along the way, and meetings teach us many lessons in life. If we keep our eyes and ears open and observe the society around us, we can get many lessons based on experience. Then, we will be able to see things no one has noticed earlier. It will help us to become more compassionate to the needy.

Although I travel by car and airplanes today, in the early days, my vehicle to go to my office and to the radio studio was first a bicycle, then a small moped, a two-wheeler.

I like bicycles, then and now. Once, my motorcycle overturned. It skidded and fell. My leg, pressed against its silencer, got burned. It was very painful. There was no other damage. After that incident, my people forced me to buy a car.

One day, I was going from Niranam to Thiruvalla to record a radio talk. I liked the sights along the wayside. Some of the notable sights in the morning were of schoolchildren walking to school, milkmen carrying pails of milk on their bicycles, newspaper boys riding bicycles and distributing papers, etc. How marvellous were the flowers, trees, the river and the city itself!

Along the way, I saw a man lying by the roadside. He was covered with a soiled sheet. The surroundings were also dirty. As the car moved ahead, I told the driver, 'Stop the vehicle.'

He reduced the speed and brought it to a halt slightly ahead.

Silently, he turned his head, meaning to ask what I wanted.

'Reverse it back a bit more. There's a man lying there,' I said.

'Oh! Maybe, he's dead. If we go and look, a police case and other troubles could follow,' he cautioned.

'Never mind. Let's see.'

He drove the car backwards. There he was, lying on the ground. A skeleton of a man covered in flies, with ants nibbling at him.

I stepped out of the car. Sensing our presence, the flies hovered up and away with a buzz. The appalling stench was disquieting. I uncovered his sheet a wee bit. My God! He was alive. He was trying to open his eyes set in deep sockets. A feeble groan could be heard.

He seemed to be a traveller or a beggar. There was a bandaged wound on his leg. His eyelashes were covered by a thick yellow and sticky film. He tried to move, but could not.

A few more people who knew me now gathered around.

'He has been lying here for two days now,' one of them said.

In fact, I wanted to ask, 'Then, shouldn't you have been more compassionate and taken him to a hospital?' But I did not. Most people are generally like that. Even if someone lay there dead, nobody would care.

'He's alive. Let's take him to the hospital,' I said.

'If something happens to him, we'll be made answerable. Let the police or someone else come and take charge,' another onlooker suggested.

'No,' I told the driver: 'Let's get him into the car. We'll take him to a hospital.'

Together, everyone lifted him and put him in the back seat of the car.

I took him to a private hospital at Thiruvalla and ensured that he would get good treatment. I agreed to pay his hospital bill.

After reaching the office, I informed the police about it. He survived. After getting better, he left the hospital. (I think the man died) His whereabouts are unknown today. I do not know who that ant-eaten man was. But I was certain that he was a human being, a man who wanted to live. How did he end up like that? He also would have a story to tell. But there's nobody even to listen to it. I too haven't heard his story. Let him live. That is all I want.

Not only human beings, but trees are also dear to me. I am convinced that the presence of trees ensures man's survival on the face of the planet earth. I do not like even to cut the branches of trees. They should grow up, waving their branches majestically in the air. Birds should build their nests on them. And I will rest under the pleasant shade of their cool, expansive greenery.

There was a hitch when our building was being built. Two trees in front of the planned building were earmarked to be felled in order to build the new seven-storey structure. As I had instructed that no trees should be cut for the new building, the engineer informed me. I visited the site.

Awaiting the death warrant were a noseberry tree (Chikoo/ Sapota), and a jackfruit tree that bore round-shaped jackfruit. I looked at them. It seemed to me that they were pleading, 'Please don't execute us.'

'Re-draft the plan, retaining these trees,' I instructed the architect.

They did so. Both those trees were standing in front of our building alive and well. They must have said time and again 'thank you . . . for allowing us to live' by fluttering their leaves and nodding their crowns whenever I passed by.

We need trees, plants and those flowing rivers and streams for our healthy life. Today we are all experiencing the ill-effects of felling trees and killing rivers. Whenever I come across good trees or medicinal herbs during my travels, I buy them and plant them in our community. Today, the 180-acre community where our Synod Secretariat is situated is a large garden. My travels taught me to be as good to humans as to plants.

Nobody likes to visit unclean places during travels. It is natural, and not a fault. I have been inspired, though, by the life and philosophy of St Teresa of Calcutta (Mother Teresa), the mother of the poor, who went seeking and caring for destitute people sleeping in the streets of Calcutta.

A few months ago, I visited Delhi. After my official business, I went to a slum along with my fellow-workers. I went there looking for a possibility to educate the little children who are deprived of educational opportunities. The small houses on either side of the narrow streets resembled those in the sprawling Dharavi slum in Mumbai. Many of those were only single-room houses with tin-sheet walls and plastic-sheet roofs. The loose concrete slabs covering dirty open sewer lines lay scattered around. Black-coloured sewage flowed like a stream. Huts were situated on both flanks of those sewage streams. Little children ran around naked or semi-naked. Most of them did not go to school.

Walking along that narrow alley, we reached a small hut. We had to bend and bow our heads to enter it through a small hole that functioned as the door. A Hindi-speaking man who accompanied me entered the house through that door covered with a piece of an old sari hanging like a curtain. He was familiar with them. He called us inside.

In the dim light, I saw a mother and her beautiful little daughter. There was no one else there. The mother greeted us by joining her palms together. I responded. She told us in Hindi how her husband had passed away, and how her ill-health prevented her from going to work. She could not send the little girl to school. Dark clouds of grief lurked in her eyes. I took the little girl in my hands. She was not at ease when I carried her.

'What's your name?' I asked, looking into her eyes.

'Nandita,' she said in a shy tone.

'Lovely name.'

'Mmm.'

'Did you eat?'

She shook her head, signifying 'No.'

I became sad. I sighed heavily and told her mother: 'From today, she is my daughter.'

She looked at me in surprise.

'All these people standing here are working with me. I shall be taking care of everything concerning my daughter Nandita. I will bear all her educational expenses. You should not be worried about anything. God bless you,' I said.

The mother's eyes sparkled. Her lips began to quiver. She bent forward and touched my feet, thanking me.

I put Nandita down on the floor, touched her head and stood silently praying for the blessings of God. She stood still with her palms joined together. I left after instructing my fellow workers in Delhi to do everything for that little girl.

My journey continues. And so do the sights along the way. I travel hoping to brighten with goodness and compassion each and every opportunity that life brings before me. Let us do all the good we can for those in need while we have the opportunity to do so. Look for any opportunity to show kindness, this is God-given privilege. Don't neglect it.

Your life has been tough and hard, but please know, help is on the way. You will make it.

7

Waiting for a Good Word

In the year 1746, a prolific British statesman, Philip Stanhope in his letter to his son wrote, 'Whatever is worth doing at all, is worth doing well and nothing can be done well without attention.' This letter along with several other letters was published in 1774 which became a huge motivating factor for millions around the world.[1]

This is a principle that one should apply in one's work field. Whenever we engage in any activity, we must ask ourselves, 'Why am I doing this? If it is worthwhile, am I doing it in the best possible manner?'

Nothing is more deplorable than half-heartedly doing a job that one does not like. We must make it a habit to like the things we do. If the job or service we are doing can make a difference in the lives of others, then we should do that to the best of our abilities.

The secret behind the success of my radio programme 'Spiritual Journey' for over three decades is that I knew it was influencing people and making a difference in their lives. What inspires us to continue the work we are doing is the realization that it is causing millions to find hope and new beginning in life.

I remember how a girl from a remote northern part of Kerala once wrote to me:

She wrote, 'Problems have so overwhelmed me that it's impossible for me to live. Everyone keeps me at a distance. If I make a small mistake, they exaggerate it and spread it around in an adverse manner to cause me calumny. I don't want to live any longer. But I felt that I must tell you about it.

'What should I do? I will wait for four more days from the date of receipt of this letter. Please send me a reply in writing or through radio. If I don't get a response after four days, I will end my life in suicide.'

The girl's name and address was written at the bottom of this letter. Fortunately, I was able to read the letter right on the day I received it. My heart stood still for a moment as I finished reading it.

Here is a girl who is determined to take her own life. She has some hope in me. But what can I do?

I wished I could meet her in person, but that was just not possible. Neither was it feasible to find a solution to her problems through radio talk and counselling. Because the regular practice was to prepare each week's programme in advance and send it to the radio station. The listeners were not aware of this, and so they would think it was a spontaneous talk. There was only one option left—to write a reply letter and post it without loss of time.

I quickly took a paper and began to write:

'Dear Kumari, I am in receipt of your letter. No one on this earth can destroy you except yourself. And there is no problem on earth that doesn't have a solution. You have a future. And I am praying to God for you.'

I signed the letter with my name and arranged to dispatch it by Speed Post. Along with the letter we sent her some other written materials that would be a help to her.

I prayed that this letter should reach her within three days. I realized one thing—that the matter I got involved in was not trivial. A human life facing destruction was right in front of me. And I had the responsibility to handle the situation. If I were a wee bit late, the casualty would be a valuable life.

Although I felt gratified that this young girl had placed her trust in me, I felt a shudder and a flash of fear within me. One, two, three, four . . . the days passed by. It was a week now and still there was no news. 'O God, please . . . May nothing happen to this girl,' I kept praying during my hours of prayer.

After three weeks, one day as I walked into our office, I found a mother and her daughter waiting for me in the lobby. They stood up as soon as I entered. I slowed down and halted on seeing them. The girl ran towards me, saying: 'It's me! (she told her name).' She bent down and touched my feet. By then her mother also joined us.

'Your letter saved me. I am so grateful,' she said.

'It's all due to piling up of unnecessary thoughts and worries. Anyway, through prayers, we got back my daughter's life,' added her mother. 'We got to know all about this only two days after we received your letter.'

I felt relieved. Thank God she didn't take her own life. I prayed with them and bid them goodbye. It was a moment that reinforced my conviction about the value of what we do to serve the needy around us.

Here is another episode from those days:

I was reading a book when the phone rang. I picked up the receiver, told my name, and asked who was at the other end. A man, who seemed to be greatly troubled, spoke, 'Sir, I want to meet you. My wife is annoyed with me. Please help me. Sir, will you please talk to her?'

I told him to come with his wife to our office the next day. Accordingly, both of them promptly came to me on the following day.

They got married twelve years ago. As I listened to their story, it seemed to me that their conjugal life was about to end. His wife was named Asha. She said, 'You may say what you like! But I cannot live with this man anymore. These twelve years of my married life have been a virtual hell. Whatever I do, he keeps scolding me. I have had nothing but blistering experiences.'

I asked her, 'What changes would you expect in your husband, so you can continue to live together?'

She replied: 'This man is the worst husband in the world. He constantly keeps bashing me, treating me cruelly, and scolding me. What's the use of my living such a life?'

I talked to both of them at length. Finally, the husband spoke these words, which still remain fresh in my memory: 'Only now I have realized how much I have pained my wife. And I have just understood the immense loss that occurred as I treated her despicably without even giving her the basic value of a human being.'

I asked him, 'Do you now wish to change your life and conduct, and really make your family life enriched and happy?'

'Absolutely,' he replied, bowing his head. Both of them apologised to each other and left joyfully.

Once, as we were travelling to Idukki, we stopped by the wayside to have a drink of water. Down below in the steep slope of the hill, we perceived a thatched hut. Seeing us, a twelve-year-old boy came out of the hut and climbed up towards us.

He wore small knickers. With almost all the buttons gone, he tried to stuff most of it into his side. He had nothing else to put on. When he approached us, I asked him, 'What's your name?'

He told us his name. For a while, we continued to chat with him. Midway, I asked him: 'Hey, do you have a radio at home?'

'Yes.'

'Which programmes do you listen to?'

He replied: 'In the morning we listen to the radio programme 'Athmeeya Yathra'. I became interested in his conversation. I felt glad thinking that, after all, he was one of my young listeners.

But I did not tell him that I was the speaker he was listening to. Instead, I asked him things like 'What are you studying?' Who all are listening to 'Athmeeya Yathra' and so on. And then we went on our way.

It was encouraging to know that my teaching was being heard even by those homes where I was unable to go myself, and it resided in the hearts of little children. However, for a while, I felt guilty for not revealing my identity to that boy.

Once I went to a college to talk to the students. It was at a university with over 1,600 students. I spent about an hour there.

I was there to talk on the topic 'How should we live in this century? When we are faced with problems, how can we lead a winning life?' I sat with a few Professors and some of my friends there, and had some coffee. Thereafter, we went around their departments. Then a boy approached me and said, 'Can I talk to you for just five minutes?' I told him to wait there for a few minutes till I was back, and I moved forward with them. Shortly, I returned and spoke to that boy. I asked his name, and inquired what his problem was. He replied, 'I often listen to your Spiritual Journey Radio programme.'

He continued with the story of his own home—very sad and disheartening experiences. He said:

'My father was my greatest enemy. We would never once talk, looking at each other face to face. It's been two years since I came here to study. A few weeks back, my daddy wrote me a letter mentioning that, having heard your Spiritual Journey talks, he has had a change of heart and a new life.'

I asked him to share what his father had written to him. He explained: 'My father had never once said anything good about me or a good word throughout his life. But in the letter, he wrote about my many good qualities and virtues, and at the end of it all, he asked me to forgive him.' As I was leaving after attending the meeting arranged there, the words of this young man kept resounding in my ears.

In those days there were hundreds of such experiences. To this day, I have been able to take active part in social service and awareness campaigns only by virtue of the fact that the work we do helps renew the society, and many people return to a renewed life.

Our lives should become valuable. We must do our work whole-heartedly. Countless are the people that are waiting to hear a good word, and to experience kindness in word and deed.

Encouragement is the oxygen of our soul; we die on the inside without it. Say something nice to at least one person a day. Begin at your home.

8

The Sins of the Saint

'If you want to see the brave, look at those who can forgive.'[1]

Stray Birds, a collection of poems written by Rabindranath Tagore (1861-1941), author of *Gitanjali*, has a little poem with the following verse (184):

'He who is too busy doing good finds no time to be good.'[2]

In this context, I remembered what a saint wrote about the plight of man who does evil despite his desire to do good.[3] Man's ego leads him away from his innate nature to love and forgive.

One evening, as I was immersed in such readings and musings, I came across an imaginative story from ancient Kerala that closely reflected the fable I read from Lewis B

Smedes' book, 'Forgive and Forget', the views of Tagore and the Saint I mentioned earlier.

Once upon a time there lived a grocer who was so 'fair and just' that people called him 'Pharisee'. He was conceited by the thought that he was more just, good, righteous, and faultless than others. But his 'own righteousness' did not let him do any good or help to anyone else.

Owing to his heartless disposition, he also had the habit of denigrating and talking ill of others. His conversation would always be laced with comments like 'Look, I am not like that' or 'Learn from me' or 'See how I am'.

Pharisee's wife was named 'Frailty.' Tall and heavy built, she would be dressed in a frilled single dhoti called mundu and a full-length blouse called chatta along with a long white towel. The whole outfit actually made her look stouter.

She would rise early and prepare food for her husband before he went to work at dawn. She would pack his lunch in a banana leaf lightly sautéed over the fire. And then she used to spend the whole day looking after her household chores and children. Saint would return home only late in the evening.

Seventeen years had passed since their marriage. Saint never once uttered a word of thanks or love to his wife. And so she lived in solitude all these years. She would often sit alone and cry.

The only comfort Frailty had was the time she found now and then to talk to the man staying in her neighborhood. They became intimate friends.

One day, by chance Pharisee returned home at noon. As he entered, what he saw filled him with rage: Frailty and the neighbour lying together on the bed!

The episode became the talk of the town. Everyone thought that Pharisee would give a sound thrashing to his wife and renounce her. What else could such a self-righteous man do in this case! But the Pharisee told the folks that he had forgiven his wife all her deeds. And he found himself justified by thinking that he was not, after all, a cruel man as the others reckoned him to be.

From that day onward, Pharisee began to sleep alone in a separate room. While he had rarely spoken to her in the past, now he would not even utter a word to her. And he stopped looking at her either. Anger and animosity kept growing within him. With increasing bitterness, he hated Frailty who had caused him such dishonour.

However, fearing what the community would speak about him, he was not prepared to abandon her. But the divorce had indeed already taken place within his heart. His hatred kept growing day after day, even as a cobra's venom keeps getting stronger with time.

Although people could not gauge Pharisee's inner broodings, his own guardian angel 'Niobe' kept regularly updating God with everything. God commanded Niobe to impose the punishment given to those who refrain from forgiveness.

Accordingly, every time Pharisee dealt with his wife in rancour, the links of an iron chain would fasten around his neck. Tiny iron links began to increase in number day after day. His shoulders began to stoop from pain and the weight of the chain. The growing burden only nourished his hatred and bitterness.

Like the growing tentacles of a purple yam, Pharisee's body began to be entwined in the chain. Finding it hard to walk upright, he began to stoop like a hunchback. He needed the support of a walking stick to venture out of the house. He wished to die rather than live in that condition.

By now Pharisee's face had begun to exhibit a dark hue, and he looked much older than his years. Bitterness and rancour turned Saint into a cruel man.

It became his daily routine to torture his wife. 'You adulteress, it's because of you that I've been reduced to this state. I lost my job. And due to your sins, God's punishment has come upon me,' he would say, and keep wounding Frailty with words sharper than double-edged sword. She was helpless, and could do nothing but cry.

One dark night Pharisee's guardian angel Niobe appeared before him. He told him a way to get rid of the chain that had fastened upon him, and to be freed from his hunch.

'There's only one way,' the angel said. 'You must forgive your wife from the bottom of your heart. Don't look upon her as a woman who cheated you, but see her as one who earnestly loved you and desperately yearned for your love. Forgiveness alone is the way to your healing and freedom.'

Pharisee replied: 'She's a sinner. None can correct the wrongs she has done.'

Guardian angel continued: 'You're not wrong. She is at fault. But if only you forgive her, you can wipe away the wounds, pain, and bondage that you have suffered on account of your unforgiveness.'

Finally, Pharisee asked Niobe what he must do in order to forgive from the bottom of his heart.

Instantaneously the angel took Pharisee into a large room that looked like a cinema hall. A couple of dim bulbs were burning here and there. The angel seated Pharisee upon a chair and commanded 'START'. Immediately a movie began to play on the screen in front. It was titled 'This Was Your Life'.

Within a few moments, Pharisee realized that it was his own life story: the house where he was born and brought up, childhood days, playing with his friends, and what not; even highly secret things that none but he only knew . . . he was seeing all these on the screen! Stealing money from his dad's wallet; telling lies; swearing falsely in God's name to escape punishment; having an affair with a girl and later ditching her when he found out she was pregnant; being dishonest in his business, and what not—he began to see all these things upon the screen.

Every now and then Pharisee would scream: 'Enough! Enough! Don't show me anymore . . .'

Guardian angel replied: 'No choice. You have to see.'

Finally he saw a horrible place that was burning with raging fires. 'That's hell. And that's where you are going,' said the angel.

Pharisee kept screaming: 'No . . . No . . . I don't want to go there. I don't want to go there.'

The angel said, 'The only way to escape is to acknowledge your plight and seek forgiveness of your sins and forgive others.'

Pharisee had a conversion of heart. He asked God for forgiveness and mercy.

Having seen Pharisee's change of heart, the angel said to him: 'Merciful God has forgiven you your sins. Now go and forgive Frailty. Don't forget that you are yourself in need of forgiveness.'

Pharisee ran back home and hugged his wife Frailty. He narrated all that had happened. He forgave her everything, and they opened a new chapter in their life.

Pharisee regained love, joy, complete health and freedom. They lived thus happily ever after.

Many of those who appear to be good have a secret life of their own. Many are those who live with a mask. Their true personality is different. In order to get over this dichotomy, we need to fear God and cry out for His mercy.

The story of Pharisee roused my inner self. Who has the right to judge or condemn another? I was, more than ever, convinced that we need to surrender ourselves to God's mercy and walk in the ways of love and forgiveness.

Live in forgiveness. Give yourself permission to do so.

9

An Elixir for Freedom

'The man who foolishly does me wrong, I will return to him that protection of my most ungrudging love, and the more evil comes from him, the more good shall go from me.'

Buddha, C. 561 – 483 B.C[1]

There was a knock at my door. I said, 'Come in.' There walks in Manoj who was working in our Headquarters. Manoj was tall and lanky, with a wheat complexion. His brunet hair was dishevelled and fallen all over his forehead.

He stood facing me, and I greeted him at once: 'Hi Manoj, welcome. You look good. Come, sit down.' He walked up to me, bowing his head and I placed my hand on his forehead and said, 'God bless you.'

He said 'Thanks' and tried to smile as he sat down.

I looked into his eyes—glittering eyes with white pupils. He wore a loose T-shirt with graffiti in bold letters running from chest to stomach that read, 'I WILL MAKE YOU FREE'. Manoj looked at me. I laughed and said:

'Go on, Manoj. How are you?'

He looked at me again, and made a vain attempt to smile. There was a look of helplessness in his eyes.

'I can't get along with these people here. What should I do?' Manoj came to the point. I know Manoj was a straight shooter.

'No one likes what I tell them. And so they keep me out from several things. It's hard for me to pull on this way.' It occurred to me that Manoj was on the verge of quitting his job.

'Manoj,' I replied. 'Look, you are a smart young man. You are loved by a lot of people, even if you don't know that.'

'That's all fine,' said Manoj. 'But . . .' His voice cracked and trailed off. Now the blue veins on his neck stood up.

After a brief silence I asked him to share his problems with me. Perhaps, when one shares problems and knows that the other is listening, it gives some peace and relief from tension. I had a little knowledge about the psychology of persons with mental disturbances.

Now, only the low noise of the air conditioner in the room was audible. Manoj simply rolled his eyes upward and then looked at me. And he began to talk. As he narrated in detail the things that had happened ever since he came to work in our office, his body language made it clear to me that the problem was with him, and not with the others.

After having listened to his story at length, I asked him: 'Can you tell me where you lived and worked before you landed here? And what happened there?' This is what I gathered from Manoj's conversation: In his previous job, Manoj had been working under a very harsh supervisor. A host of problems cropped up with this supervisor. As those difficulties did not find a resolution, the roots of bitterness began to grow in his heart. And the memories of the happenings at the previous location still keeps haunting and hurting him.

'Beware of bitterness that has gone deep into you. Else, it can hurt your inside and many others you associate with,' I cautioned him.

His actual problem was not related to what he spoke in his dealings with his co-workers. An unforgiving heart, memories that he could not let go of, painful experiences, hatred, vengeance—all of these helped the root of bitterness to go deep into his life.

Any extent of talking with him would not have brought up a real solution to his problems. They could only be resolved by understanding the actual problems that lay hidden within his subconscious self. I felt glad that on that occasion I was able to understand those underlying things, to talk to him about it and resolve his problems, and thereby to make his life enriched.

As he wiped his tears in joy and stood up to go, the graffiti on his T-shirt caught my attention once again: 'I WILL MAKE YOU FREE'.

'Manoj, this is amazing!' I told him. 'God's message for you is already in your possession.'

Manoj looked at his T-shirt like a child and stood up. Flashing an innocent smile, he said, 'Thank you.'

Manoj continued with us for many more years. Some hurts that he found it hard to forgive had become roots of bitterness within him and were destroying him like slow poison. When we found a remedy for it, he was set free.

We cannot overcome unforgiving memories through education or money power. Unforgiving memories are subtle villains that reside in one's subconscious mind. They fill one's life with the venom of bitterness. And they kill one's confidence and competence to lead an active life.

Let me now share with you the experiences of Sudha, a girl who used to regularly listen to my radio talks.

Her father was an alcoholic right from the days of her early childhood. There was not a day when he wouldn't get drunk. Sudha grew up seeing her dad constantly floundering in the illusory land of intoxication.

He was a Maths teacher at the nearby high school. Apart from that, he was a party activist too. Sudha was his eldest daughter. She had three younger siblings.

He would come home, fully drunk and disoriented, at about 2.00 a.m. or 3.00 a.m. in the wee hours of the night. As a result of his harassment, Sudha's mother became ill and bed-ridden. The household responsibilities thus fell on twelve-year-old Sudha's shoulders. This little girl had to take over all the household tasks and burdens, such as nursing her mother, looking after the siblings, cooking their food, and so on.

Years passed on in this manner. Sudha was now seventeen years of age. One night her father came home fully drunk, along with one of his friends. The visitor attempted to rape Sudha. She immediately raised an alarm, and fortunately escaped unhurt on that day.

She was greatly distressed at her father's alcoholism and abominable behaviour. Although heart-broken, she continued her education and completed her college-level studies. Then she got married.

She lived a happy life for a few weeks. And then problems cropped up with her husband. Her life became much like the proverbial 'from the frying pan to the fire' situation.

Sudha was mentally broken and physically worn out. She became mum, listless, and interested in nothing at all. Her life drifted from brokenness to brokenness. She attempted suicide twice.

Through the intervention of an uncle, she was taken for psychiatric treatment that stretched to several months. Many an expert psychiatrist counselled and treated her. At the end of it all, one day she erupted like a volcano and shouted: 'I hate him. I hate him.'

And who is this man she hated so much? That's her own father who killed her mother; who dealt with her in a cruel and abominable manner; who ruined her future; who killed her zest; a man who smashed her dignity and interest in life.

That was her own drunkard father who had created circumstances that compelled her to forego the joys of childhood and to take up household responsibilities; a man who paved the way to smash her mind and body to smithereens . . . 'I hate him,' she kept shouting this a hundred times.

The doctors detected her problem. Anger, hatred, and thoughts of vengeance kept nibbling at her soul—not for a year or two, but several years. But those psychiatrists were unable to heal her.

By now her father, who had persisted with his alcoholism, finally ended up as a patient and got admitted to a hospital. She had not seen her dad's face for over three years. Had she seen it, she would certainly have lost her sleep during the weeks that followed. As such, she had no desire to see her father. And thus he died.

At this juncture, one of her girlfriends gave her a copy of the Holy Scripture for reading. As she was reading, the teachings of Christ that said, 'Love your enemies; forgive . . . don't seek vengeance'[2] and so on touched her heart. From that day a new perspective entered into her heart.

Meanwhile, one day she happened to hear my radio talk concerning forgiveness. And she realized that the solution to all her problems lay in her own hands. She must forgive her dad. Otherwise, she would not get healed. But then there was a problem—her father was no more.

'What shall I do now?' she asked herself.

Without wasting any more time, she rose and picked up a paper and a pen, and began to write a letter along these lines:

Dear Daddy,

I have given up my bitterness and anger towards you forever. I have forsaken all the painful memories, sentiments, and hateful thoughts that I have been keeping in my mind since my childhood. I am fortunate in my life to understand the mercy of God to all people. I have read in Holy Scripture we should not live with hatred and without forgiving. And so I have forgiven all the wrongs that Daddy did to me.

I have often wondered as to why Daddy had become such a cruel man. How did Daddy become a person filled with so much bitterness, who could not love or reciprocate love? Perhaps Daddy, you had some love in your heart, or a loving and generous heart at some time or other. But I was not lucky enough to see that good aspect anytime.

When Daddy was lying sick in the hospital, I did not have the courage to come and meet you. That's because I hated you so much then.

I didn't want to come for your funeral. However, I did make an appearance as I feared others' opinion.

Next Thursday is Daddy's birthday. I will go to Daddy's tomb on that day. I know pretty well that the very thought of your absence will be painful to me.

Daddy, this pain is not from anger or bitterness. But rather, it stems from love. For the first time in my life, I have known freedom. I have been liberated as I forgave.

Rest in peace, Daddy.

With loving kisses,
Your daughter,
Sudha.

She wrote this letter and kept it at her father's grave.

It was a year later that she came to meet me after this episode. Her face was radiant with the light of freedom and joy that forgiveness had given her.

It is possible that, just like Sudha, your heart might have been broken at times due to the dealings and demeanour of others. Maybe you are living in grief and pain. You may be diseased and a patient. But there is a solution to your problem. Forgive from the bottom of your heart, and forget. And you will experience freedom and healing right here and now.

You must have heard about kidnappers who abduct others. If you comply with the demands that they notify over phone, letters or bulletins, then they will release the kidnapped person. Their demand is, 'Give us what we ask, and we'll let them go.'

When we fail to forgive the wrongs that others do to us, we are doing no better than they. Please don't misunderstand me, I am not suggesting that you are a kidnapper. But the truth is that right now you have withheld the love, acceptance, honour, kindness, generosity, forbearance, charity, etc., that is due to them. In other words, you have snatched them away. You are denying them their rights.

So, aren't you saying this? 'You have troubled me. You have done me wrong. I have been hurt. You must suffer punishment until you do reparation. You must also suffer pain. Henceforth you will not get love, acceptance, honour, etc., from me. I have kept you far from me.'

Don't forget what we reflected upon in the previous chapter. The meaning of 'forgiveness' is to write off all the debts in full.

They are your debtors. They wilfully hurt you. But you must whole-heartedly and willingly let it go. You must take away that wrong from the wrongdoer. If you don't do that, you are only trying to protect your own interest, even as kidnappers do. In that case, you would be the real loser as you haven't forgiven others.

Bitterness is a deadly poison while forgiveness is an elixir. Most of the diseases that we suffer from today can be healed simply through forgiveness.

Examine yourself and see if you have any painful experiences of old, or hurtful memories. It may be that in your subconscious mind you are harbouring some bitterness or hatred towards your father, mother, wife, or husband. And you may be able to live without letting anyone else know. But you must know that as time moves on, the roots of bitterness will grow and overpower you. Forgive today . . . Write that letter or make that phone call now. And then you will see the heaven of freedom opening right before your eyes.

God does not forget us sinners, He forgets our sins— forever.

10

The Beauty of Ugliness

On that day, I set off for Wayanad early in the morning. Wayanad is a north-eastern district in Kerala. Historically, Wayanad is believed to have evolved from 'wayal nadu' or 'the land of paddy fields.' Wayanad consists of mountain ranges of the Western Ghats. The mountains there range from 700 to 2,100 metres in height. The Banasura Hill is the tallest. Wayanad is also home to a temple dedicated to Luv-Kush (legendary twin sons of Lord Rama) and the Temple of Mirrors, a Jain place of worship. One must ascend the meandering ghat road from Kozhikode (Calicut) in order to reach Wayanad, the land filled with nature's captivating bounty and beauty.

I travelled by train up to Kozhikode (six-hour-long journey). From there onward it was a road trip. Travelling so far by car from Thiruvalla would have been arduous as I was scheduled to speak at a meeting.

Our car began to ascend the ghat road early in the morning. As we negotiated a couple of hairpin bends of the road that lay like a twisted python, I felt as though my eardrums were shutting down; that's a common experience for those going up along the ghat roads. The mountain crevices were filled with mist-like rising smoke. At some places, we could see the mountain peaks touching the sky with the misty clouds.

The meeting was at Sulthan Bathery. The organizers had gone ahead on the previous day. A member of the organizing committee had arranged his house to be used for our rest. As we arrived, a girl and her mother were waiting for us, having heard about our visit.

Both of them approached me with folded hands. The girl was lean and thin, and her complexion dark as pitch. Her eyes were dull and listless. Her mother stood by with a doleful face, like a withered flower.

'Sir, please pray for her. You must speak to her for a few minutes,' insisted the mother.

'What's the problem?'

'Nobody likes me. Blackie . . . Crowie . . . people call me such names,' she sobbed. Without looking at me, she continued: 'It's because of this taunting . . . that I decided to die.'

I looked at her mother. She stood with folded hands, like a bird that has lost its wings.

'My mother saw it, and saved me,' the girl added.

'How old are you?' I asked.

'Twenty-two.'

'How far did you study?'

'Plus Two. And I can also stitch dresses.'

'Child, you have a beautiful complexion. God created you. He is your master. Don't ever listen to what anyone else says. God will give you a very bright future,' I said and saw a glow of light on her mother's countenance. The girl did not utter a word. She kept standing, not knowing what to do.

'My girlfriends keep taunting me, saying things like 'Who will marry you?'

'Bad luck to the boy who marries you' . . . and so on. That's the time I think of killing myself,' she said and kept sobbing. She wiped her tears with the edge of her faded churidar.

I kept talking to them for a little while longer. I boosted her self-confidence by asserting that she was indeed good-looking, and that what others were saying about her was not true. I laid my hand on her shoulder and prayed for her. I deliberately chose words of love and hope that the Holy Scripture speaks of God's love and acceptance of her, the creation of God. They left joyfully.

Some tribal kids were busy playing on the mud tracks nearby. They wore either a short little cotton towel or knickers. I had heard that several tribal clans such as Adiyas, Paniyas, Kurichiyans, Kattunayakans, etc., lived in Wayanad. Whatever their clans, they are all human beings . . . children of God . . . such were the thoughts that passed through my mind.

As I was descending down the ghat road after my meeting in Wayanad, I kept remembering the dark girl and praying that good things might happen to her.

And then I recollected concerning an extraordinary letter that a woman had written to me. A physically challenged woman, she was married, and her letter read:

'Sir, I am disabled with a limp on my leg. When I was at school, my friends used to constantly mock me. I could do nothing but sit whimpering in a corner and cry. This would happen many times over.

'I was despondent and broken. What devastated me further was that my father and mother used to call me 'Hey, Limper!' and scold me. With that, I lost the little self-esteem I had.

'Around this time, my marriage took place. He knew pretty well about my disability when he married me. I used to often keep thinking as to why he never once asked me about my limp. Being curious to know about my husband's thoughts on this, I once asked him, "You know I keep limping. People keep mocking when they see me."

'Immediately my husband called me to his side and said. "No, never talk such things. God has created you with a great purpose. I love you deeply just as you are. As far as I am concerned, you are the most beautiful woman in the world." Hearing these words, I burst into tears.

'It's been twenty-one years since we got married. There's not a single thing that I haven't done for my husband. I love him so much.'

Her own parents used to be contemptuous to her. And her friends would taunt her. But her husband became willing to accept her as she was, and to love her. With that, her self-confidence multiplied manifold. And she was able to lead a joyful life. St Teresa of Calcutta once said, 'The biggest disease today is not leprosy or tuberculosis, but rather the feeling of being unwanted.'[1] Those who mock physically challenged persons actually suffer from mental abnormality. People who do not feel sympathy toward fellow beings have an inhuman nature.

Believe it or not, world-renowned plastic surgeons testifying, even after the most face is re-created by the skilled hand of the surgeon, the changed, converted— now beautiful face don't change the self-rejection, people maintained in their subconscious. You may be most handsome or beautiful person on the outside, but on the inside you live with rejection and self-hate. That most probably happened through the negative words others have said about you—could be your family member, teachers and friends. The way of healing is and out is by accepting yourself for, God loves and accepts you. There are many good books you can read about this subject. It is worth doing it.

By now our car had descended from the ghat. We reached Kozhikode and continued our journey by train.

Sometime back I happened to read a story. 'A store owner was tacking a sign above his door that read 'Puppies For Sale.' Signs like that have a way of attracting small children, and sure enough, a little boy appeared under the store owner's sign, 'How much are you going to sell the puppies for?' he asked.

The store owner replied, 'Anywhere from $30 to $50.'

The little boy reached in his pocket and pulled out some change. 'I have $2.37,' he said. 'Can I please look at them?'

The store owner smiled and whistled and out of the kennel came Lady, who ran down the aisle of his store followed by five teeny, tiny balls of fur. One puppy was lagging considerably behind. Immediately the little boy singled out the lagging, limping puppy and said, 'What's wrong with that little dog?'

The store owner said, 'No, you don't want to buy that little dog. If you really want him, I'll just give him to you.'

The little boy got quite upset. He looked straight into the store owner's eyes, pointing his finger, and said, 'I don't want you to give him to me. That little dog is worth every bit as much as all the other dogs and I'll pay full price. In fact, I'll give you $2.37 now and 50 cents a month until I have him paid for.'

The store owner countered, 'You really don't want to buy this little dog. He is never going to be able to run and jump and play with you like the other puppies.'

To this, the little boy reached down and rolled up his pant leg to reveal a badly twisted, crippled left leg supported by a big metal brace. He looked up at the store owner and softly replied, 'Well, I don't run so well myself, and the little puppy will need someone who understands!'[2]

Only those who suffer pain can really understand the pain and weaknesses of others who are experiencing similar suffering. Their own disability becomes an inspiration for them to know and help others who have limitations like themselves.

When we realize that God is the creator of everyone, then we will be able to accept and love everyone. Love has no place for colour or comeliness. We must accept one another for our own good.

While our physical eyes see all the good and bad, the inner eyes of our soul will see the beautiful hidden handiwork of the Creator, if only we pause and think.

11

Memories of My Village

I am looking back at the memories of Niranam area forty years ago. Niranam is the village where I was born and brought up.

In those days, roads and electric power lines were few and far between. Almost all houses depended on kerosene lamps for light. Everyone went around on foot. A bus used to come around just once a day. We had to walk quite a long distance to board that bus. But in those days, there was peace and tranquillity in human lives. If there was a death, all the people in the village would rush to that house and share in the sorrow.

I remember my childhood, walking to the village kindergarten nothing more than a grass hut with dirt floor. Gone are those days. Now we find the English Medium school buses plying up and down the macadamised village road from dawn to night. There is not a single house without a phone. Houses are filled with modern gadgets.

These days, if someone dies in my village, hardly five-six persons come visiting. And they will keep looking at their watch every now and then! No one has the time . . . A generation of children is now growing up that doesn't know what parental love means. Cruelty towards women is on the rise, and so are suicides.

Formerly, there was no need to lock the doors of any house in the village. But now each house has several locks!

In your childhood days, did you ever hear of the diseases that you keep hearing about today? In those days, there were only a few hospitals (for most ailments there used to be one and the same remedy. A potpourri of red-coloured medicines would be filled in a bottle, shaken, and given to the patient). You had only to drink this 'panacea' handed out by the compounder, and Presto! All your ailments would be gone in a trice—vaatham, pitham, and kabham (wind, bile, phlegm—all humours arising from the elements of air, space, fire, earth and water), the whole lot of them![1] Today, you come across 'super-specialty' hospitals at every junction! For every ailment, there is an expert specialist doctor. Diseases, however, are ever on the increase.

Today my village has become modern. Rice planting songs and harvest songs have become things of the past. Planting and harvesting machines have replaced folks and folk songs in the fields. The younger generation of harvesters have migrated to cities in search of jobs.

Previously, people used a hook and line to catch fish for making a curry. There are no such fishermen now. Instead, fish stalls have come up to sell seafood. Ferry stations have been replaced with bridges. Computers and the Internet are here. Good roads and modern cars are ubiquitous. In place of thatched houses, towering concrete structures have become the residential norm.

Notwithstanding all of the above, it is something else that makes me sad. In those days, while walking along the interior pathways at sundown, we could hear the evening prayers rising from every hutment—regardless of creed or caste. Children sporting basil flowers in their hair and vermilion applied on their foreheads after their bath at twilight standing in front of the many-tiered lamp; Syrian Christian families singing their evening hymns; mothers dressed in frilled mundu and chatta, and covering their heads with a traditional shawl (neriyathu) walking to the church for vespers . . . Gone are all these; now mere memories. These scenes have vanished not only from my village, but as much from the whole of Kerala which has embraced modernity.

Niranam of those days had very small pathways. In my childhood, it was impossible to travel by car, bus or motorbike during some seasons, especially when there were floods. All the pathways and routes would be submerged under water, and people would then travel by boats. There were a variety of boats in use—large, medium and small, beaked snake boats and even 'kothumbu vallam.'

'Kothumbu vallam' was a very small boat that could carry a single person who would keep rowing it and travel.

If a second person boarded it, it would certainly sink. There were slightly larger boats too, that could accommodate two to three passengers.

One day, at the time of the floods, my friend and I set out for school. I was no more than ten or fifteen years of age then. My friend was a bit older. We kept our school bags in the boat and began to row in the direction of our school, located about two kilometres away. The little boat kept moving forward across the waves. And we were sailing ahead with great enthusiasm and fun.

All of a sudden, the sky turned dark, and a heavy torrent of rain commenced along with gusty winds, thunder, and clouds. There was a large bund near the Thalavady school; it caved in and the floodwaters were rapidly flowing across it with a strong current. As we approached it, our boat was drawn into the current, and we were unable to steer it to safety despite our best efforts. Within a few moments our boat sank, and I fell into the water. Luckily, I escaped only because there was an older boy with me.

The memories of that day still stay fresh in my mind! Today, the situation in our village has changed a lot.

Of course, we had drunkards in our land—then and now. I can't stop laughing when I remember about their pranks. Let me share one such experience.

One night, at about 2.00 a.m., one of my schoolmates knocked at the door of my room as I slept. Greatly perturbed, I jumped out of my bed and opened the door.

My friend stood there crying, with a lantern in hand. I asked him, 'What's the matter? What happened?'

He replied: 'Every night my drunkard dad used to return home latest by 10.00 p.m. But tonight, he hasn't come home till now. We have been waiting and waiting. My mom has been awake all night, crying and saying that at this time of floods, if he slipped and fell into the water, there was no hope for him.'

I asked him, 'So, what can we do about it now?'

He said, 'Please come with me. Let's just go up to that toddy shop and enquire.'

I accompanied him. Those were the days when I even shuddered to think about his drunkard father. What was worse, we had to pass alongside the cemetery to reach there. I broke a stick from the fence and carried it to boost our courage. We walked together, carrying the lantern for light. Every now and then, my friend kept calling out, 'Daddy, Daddy.' As we came closer to the cemetery, I could feel my knees knocking against each other; nonetheless, we gathered our guts and kept going forward. My friend was still calling, 'Daddy, Daddy.'

A long-drawn humming came from the cemetery, 'Ummm . . .' I felt myself sinking, almost with a nervous breakdown. My friend called out again, 'Daddy!' The same humming again, 'Ummm . . .' We held the lantern high and looked. And there was his father, slowly rising from one of the tombstones of a grave! We helped him up and brought him out of the cemetery. We held his hand and brought him home.

We had several experiences of fellowship and goodness at Niranam.

When I was young, most of the houses in my village had no electricity. Gas stoves were unheard of; so in those days we had to light a fire at the fireplace by using a match-box. At times, we would borrow some fire from a neighbour's house if our match sticks had run out or if we had misplaced the match-box. My mother asked me to do that on several occasions.

Whenever my mother demanded, I would run to the next house with a dried coconut's outer husk in my hand. And the lady in that house would scrape out some firebrands from her oven and dump into the dry coconut husk. I would bring that home and light our oven.

Does this sound funny to you? Let me share a greater truth that such things reveal to us: They shared with us the fire that lay in their oven by transferring it to the dry coconut husk so that the fire might burn in our house as well. They did not lose anything by doing that. Instead, they merely caused a blessing—a fire was lighted in a neighbour's house!

A culture of sharing was visible in every field then. The practice of sharing food and food produce with neighbours has almost disappeared today. Food production has itself reduced. In our neighbourhood, we had a man called Unnichayan. When I was young, one day as I passed along that way, I found all the coconut trees in his 2.5-acre farm without a single coconut. The coconut trees were all standing drooped and diseased.

I asked him, 'Oh! Achaya, (that's how we address the eldest brother) how come there isn't a single coconut on those trees?'

He replied: 'Yeah! What can I do? My father doesn't give anything to Lord God. And so, God keeps taking all the coconuts upwards; nothing is coming down.'

Good enough for a hearty laugh? Yes, but therein lies some food for thought as well.

When we make offerings before God, make sure to do it willingly, and not half-heartedly and grudgingly. God has no need for our material things; nonetheless, we must faithfully handle the bounties that God bestows upon us by helping the poor and needy around us. And then we shall have prosperity. Even today, whenever I pass through Niranam, these happenings keep racing into my memory.

Remember not to forget, it will keep you safe.

12

Being Faithful in Little Things: Living for Others

This boy was sixteen years of age then. Having completed his high school, he told his mother that he wanted to help the poor and needy by joining a team of other young people going to the poor communities in difficult parts of India.

Their journey took them to Tamil Nadu, Karnataka, Maharashtra and many other states. Finally, he landed in Bombay (now Mumbai). A large conference was being hosted there. Over 300 participants from all over India had assembled there. This young boy also reached the venue to take part in this month-long conference. He had neither teaching skills nor oratorical ability. Besides, he did not know the vernacular. All in all, this boy was a 'dwarf' among the hundreds gathered there.

An idea flashed through his mind: 'God, I have none of the skills that these others have. But there's one thing I can do. The shoes and sandals of all these people gathered here are soiled with dirt and sand. When they go to bed at night, I can wipe, clean, and polish them well.'

He told his idea to one leader privately at the Conference. This supervisor said: 'Young man, that's a great idea. What would you like me to do?'

He replied: 'I need an anvil, some polish, three brushes, one cobbler's needle, some twine and wax, a hammer, and some small-sized nails.' The young man requested it would be kind enough not to tell anyone of this. He agreed.

The supervisor gave him some cash. He went and bought all those things. From 11.30 p.m. to 04.30 a.m., he sat alone in a private area in the hall way and polished hundreds of footwear and kept them neatly arranged. He did this for the whole four weeks of the conference. It remained a secret or did others know and didn't want to say anything about it. No one knows!

Who was this young man? None, but this writer. That was a small thing I could do at that time. As I was faithful in that little matter, God gave me the strength to do many more good things for others in need later in my life.

Often, we must not do good in expectation of some reward. It must flow naturally from our heart. When we see disorder and confusion, we need to have a compassionate heart in order to respond against it. We must cultivate in our minds the willingness to see others' pains as our own and reach out to them with kindness.

What the Bhagavad Gita says about nishkam karma (work without desire for reward) and the Bible says, 'Do good to others' are but one and the same—about doing good without expecting a reward or someone's appreciation. That is, doing good deeds without looking at the results of our endeavour. I learned later many of our great ancestors lived in accordance with this principle regardless of caste, creed and religion.

That small work I did acted as a spark to ignite my desire to do charitable work. For several years, I lived in the villages of North India, engaged in social service. And it acted as a buttress for me to do several projects for social uplift in later years. The inner motivation, the fire within me was the Word of Christ, 'what you have done for the least of these you have done it for me.'[1]

Once I had completed my studies in America, my heart was burning with a desire to take up some work for the development of rural people in Indian villages. Homeless people, the uneducated and illiterate, the jobless stragglers, and the sick that have no money to get treatment, those struggling to get married, hopeless leprosy patients, widows without means of sustenance, families breaking apart with problems of life, frustrated persons looking forward to suicide . . . and so on. Such were the images of people who filled my mind—those without hope, the poor and the sick, and the broken-hearted. I knew that I could not set the world right all by myself. However, I had the power to do something, even if it is just helping one person.

And that is why some friends came forward to give a helping hand. We formed a charitable organization to help the suffering people.

Through this organization, we were able to take up works of charity such as free medical services, group weddings, educational assistance and distribution of study kits, supply of work tools, relief and rehabilitation activities, and so on.

We extended the service to all corners of our nation, India. Some years later, we spread our wings to Nepal, Sri Lanka, Bangladesh, and Myanmar. Today, we are present in these nations serving the needy and hurting in our generation.

Since then, that young boy, me who had once polished shoes has found no time to rest. My life is busy with international trips, conferences and seminars, and various other tasks. Throughout my travels, I will hear of many that found hope through our mission of kindness.

In Asian countries alone, to date we were able to help 1,30,000 children to go to school and find a bright future. We are providing treatment and care to inmates of over forty leprosy colonies. I take no credit for anything we have accomplished. It's all been possible due to the kindness so many around the world, and of course God's mercy and love.

I have some painful memories that I carried back from my travels in Sri Lanka. There was a woman, about twenty-four years of age, with an emaciated body, a beautiful face, long hair that stretched down to her feet, deep-set eyes that seemed to have dried up her tears through incessant crying, and a little baby in her hands. She had delivered the child soon after the Tsunami. Her story made me sit up and ponder.

Only a day had passed since she had decided to poison herself to death after killing the child. Because she lost her parents, brothers, husband, hutment, and everything. Only one question remained—why must she live any longer? And the answer she herself found was to end her life; but not alone, she had to kill the child too.

It was at this juncture, as she kept thinking such thoughts, that our social workers happened to reach her with rice, clothes, drinking water, etc. Over 3,000 people squatted there—hopeless lives that had lost everything they had: grandparents, parents, young men and women, wives and husbands, children . . . and that woman sitting in a corner. As they approached to hand out the relief supplies, she protested, 'No . . . I don't want anything.' They asked her why. From the conversation that followed, they understood as to how her life had been reduced to such depths of desperation. However, she did not divulge her purpose and decision as yet. The workers talked to her, speaking words of comfort and consolation. They counselled her, and prayed to God to help her.

In the end, she spoke to our people and said: 'I thank you for coming and talking to me. If you hadn't come and understood my circumstances, or comforted me in my sorrow and pain, I would have ended my life tonight as I had made up my mind. I had also decided to kill my child.

But now, a ray of desire has arisen within me that, despite all these pains, losses, and desolation, I can still live with hope.'

I reached that community a day later. One of our people then told me the story of that woman. As he narrated it, his eyes filled with tears and his words stuttered with emotion.

When I travel in Sri Lanka and Nepal, I can perceive the pain hidden behind the smiles of rural children. It is the same in slums of our nation. Words cannot express the satisfaction we feel when we gather together those who suffer.

Let me share my experience when I went to Batticaloa in Sri Lanka. After my flight landed in Colombo, I had to traverse along pot-holed roads for about ten long hours before I could reach the place.

When I arrived, I found the hardship and sufferings of the people there beyond words. Over 10,000 children that have lost either one or both of their parents lived in camps.

Hundreds of Local parishes of Believers Eastern Church in Sri Lanka have come together to tirelessly strive day and night, and to love and care for those children, and to feed them. They keep preparing food and distributing water and clothes to them in the camps. They were implementing several such relief programmes . . . And that was when I reached the place.

In one such camp, there were about 400 children. When I visited another of our camps housing people who had lost everything, I met a medical doctor from America and three others along with her. The doctor's name was Mona Khanna. She looked like a Western lady.

I asked her: 'Your name doesn't sound American; does it? That's more like an Indian name?' She promptly replied: 'Your Honour, I was born and brought up in a Brahmin family in India. When I was under two years of age, my father, mother, and brother migrated to Chicago in America. My three brothers are all medical doctors. So I also studied Medicine and became a doctor.'

While matters stood thus, she began to think on these lines: 'Hey, what am I doing, making all this money? I am living a decent life. But beyond this, what can I do with my life to help others?' Such thoughts began to weigh upon her. Finally, she hit upon a decision. She resigned her job.

And then she decided to travel to many nations and help the suffering and needy people. I was amazed at the compassion of this doctor who exchanged the American dream to serve the poor.

I have come across many a person with such a sacrificing and self-denying attitude. God has touched their hearts and I am challenged by them.

In a world that has refugees, orphans, widows, the diseased, and the weeping, how could I be living only for myself? Our lives truly become enriched only when we live for others.

Life makes sense when you help others live.

13

Denying Them a Chance to Live

This happened many years ago. It was a night that stood frozen in the fury of the monsoon rains. Unmindful of the cold wind, I was going along with my friend to the Kottayam railway station. Our plan was to board the Mangalore Express. Having lost precious time waiting for an auto-rickshaw, we walked, all the while doubting whether we might miss the train. As we walked briskly, we kept talking something or other. My friend Raju suddenly said, 'Wait!' and ran towards the other side of the road.

I stood there, anxious to know what had happened, and looked in that direction. I sighted a young woman moving towards the railway tracks. By then Raju had already reached up to her. I ran and joined them. The girl was only sixteen or seventeen years of age. Her name was Rani. She had become pregnant out of wedlock. Her rain-drenched clothes revealed external signs of about five to six months of pregnancy. Unable to bear the burden of dishonour, she was running to end her life by jumping under the speeding train.

Although Raju restrained her, she kept crying bitterly, saying, 'Let me go! Let me go! Please let me die.' She made an unsuccessful attempt once to let go of our hands and rush towards the train that just whistled and passed by. Anyway, we held her fast without letting her go.

Needless to say that we missed our train and journey. However, the satisfaction of having saved a life made us cheerful. We took her along and reached Raju's house. As I had to return, I entrusted her to the care of Raju and his wife, and left.

They talked to her and learned more about her problems. Rani's parents were in the Gulf. She lived with her aged grandfather and grandmother. She became pregnant through a boy she met in college and later fell in love with. She knew pretty little about the boy.

That boy has never again been seen after her pregnancy became known. It was quite late when she became aware that she was carrying. And then she kept smouldering, not knowing what to do next. Rani recollected how hard it was for her to keep the matter under wraps and to go about as though nothing was amiss. She was amazed at how she had pulled on so far. But she couldn't go on so any longer. Her baby bump was growing bigger day by day! If she really had to deliver a child!! Oh, no! Fear engulfed her. 'I have no right to live on this earth anymore. I will put an end to this life,' she took a pledge.

And so, as her grandparents were fast asleep under the blanket, in the rain and cold, Rani quietly shut the door behind her and slipped out of the house. Had we not reached in the nick of time, that girl and the baby growing in her womb would have been crushed to death under the wheels of the train.

Raju and his wife rose to the occasion and comforted Rani, and they promised to help her. The mistake had been done. But now was the time to get over it and pick up one's life and save it. She became convinced that destroying life was not at all a solution. She felt ashamed and regretted that she had even attempted suicide. She mustered courage, and asked God for forgiveness.

They broached the matter with her grandparents without upsetting them. Her parents in the Gulf were also suitably apprised of these things. Being educated and mature, they did not fly into a rage. They realized that at this juncture it was important to help and heal her rather than blame. Raju and his family gave them all the necessary support for that.

Under the arrangements made by Raju, Rani gave birth to a lovely little boy in a charitable institution. They also took necessary steps in order to bring up the child under good care and love.

Rani found it extremely hard to separate from her child. However, in those circumstances, she could not have done otherwise. Although her studies were disrupted for about a year, she was able to make up, and continued her education with a different heart and a renewed life. And that episode became a turning point in her life.

Such a turn of events does not happen in every case. Pregnancy out of wedlock and abortion, and the resultant mental problems that they create are immensely grave.

One day in the evening, my phone began to ring. I picked it up. A lady was at the other end. She introduced herself: 'I am Mrs Susan Podil. Rev. Father, will you please come to my house?' 'Certainly,' I agreed. Along with my assistant priest, we reached the house at the scheduled time.

Mrs Susan's family received us graciously. 'I wished that you should talk to my twenty-year-old daughter. And that's why I invited you with a request,' she said.

We were introduced to her daughter Jancy, a very beautiful, educated, and unmarried young woman. However, a shade of disappointment and mental pain was visible on her face. The moment we met her, it occurred to me that she was in need of some good counselling.

We sensed that she was rather reluctant to open up her mind to us. So, her mother explained her problems thus: 'Jancy is not able to sleep well. She had great difficulty and discomfort, and would not talk to others. It has been ages since we saw a smile upon her face. She keeps sitting listlessly all the time. We took her to many hospitals, but there has been no difference. 'She was such a sweet and happy girl, always dancing around in joy. O God, whatever has happened to our child?' lamented the mother and burst into tears.

Anyway, my colleague and I decided to talk to her. But soon we realized that she was not really sharing anything openly with us. And we were troubled thinking that it would hardly be possible for us to help her unless she revealed her underlying problems before us.

However, I got inkling in my mind that I must ask her a few more specific questions. So I asked her: 'Jancy, have you ever got into an illegitimate relationship? Did you ever abort a child that was conceived in your womb?' No sooner did I ask this question than I saw her shuddering as though struck by thunder. For a few moments, her eyes were fixed vacantly somewhere in space, and then she began to cry inconsolably. Seeing her in tears, we also felt our eyes getting moist.

We waited for some time, letting her cry her heart out. When she had ceased crying, she opened up: 'I am a person who has done both. Unmarried as I was, I became pregnant. I didn't want to become an unwed mother and have a child. But that's exactly what happened. I aborted that child. And that's what has ruined my life forever. I am unable to eat or sleep or do anything else. I am scared even to go out of my room. When I am outside, if I see a little child, I get rooted to the spot. At times I keep crying or mumbling something without being aware of my surroundings. I am totally broken.'

How dreadful is the story of her pain and predicament! She might never have imagined that her illegitimate relationship would have such a tragic consequence. But the fruit of wrong choice none other.

Many are the women who have been devastated by the mental breakdown due to abortion. They are heart-broken by the feeling of guilt that they have killed an innocent child. Particularly among those who are conceiving for the first time, such a realization crushes their spirit. 'Abortion' is guilt that is beyond a woman's capability to bear physically and mentally.

Thankamma's experience illustrates this very well. Thankamma became pregnant at an unexpected time. The foetus was about ten weeks old. But Thankamma was not prepared to become a mother yet and to take care of the child so early in life. So, she resolved to abort the child, and underwent an abortion procedure at a hospital.

On that day, the people in that hospital were startled to hear a horrifying sound of loud wailing from the labour room. As the abortion procedure terminated and induced the fetus out of the womb, what came out was not a dead foetus as expected. Instead, it was alive and kicking in death throes, and seeing this partially formed and tender child, the mother broke into an ear-deafening scream. And the thought that, after all, this was the child that should have been safely growing within her added rigour to that cry. That incident shook the foundations of her psyche. And it almost made her a mental wreck. Thankamma's heart-rending scream was enough to make everyone in the hospital literally cry.

Apart from that, the psychological feeling of guilt that she was the murderer of that innocent and tender child kept haunting and destroying her inch by inch. Will not this harrowing experience keep rousing sorrowful memories in her mind till her last breath?

Here is another incident that happened in 1980:[1]

Norma was one among the attending nurses at the labour room as a 'saline abortion' procedure was being performed upon a young woman. As they were trying to expel the foetus through this procedure, what came out was a fully healthy girl child. Norma said the child was extremely beautiful.

Norma did not have the gumption to watch them pushing that tender child into the labour room basin along with the detritus and stuff that came out in the abortion process. That child had no physical infirmities. It seemed to Norma that the child, by kicking up her hands and legs as she lay in the basin, was expressing her desire to live. She kept fighting for her life by vigorously moving her limbs inside the basin.

After about six hours, under the care and responsibility of Norma and her friends, that child was shifted to the Medical Centre of Loma Linda University. After four days, they received a medical report certifying that the child was in full health, that she did not suffer any significant damage from the saline liquid, and that she could reach full growth if safely guarded and well taken care of. However, on the eleventh day, that tender child died from some other bacterial infection.

Nurse Linda's experience was no different in 1973.[2]

Following an abortion done upon a young woman, as she was trying to remove the post-operative stuff into a basin, Linda saw the child moving inside the basin. She looked at it more closely. 'I felt that the tender child was intently looking at me for mercy. I couldn't take my eyes off that tiny child whose heart was still beating. I thought that its eyes were telling me a thousand tragic stories,' said Linda in a voice heavily laden with emotions.

Linda ran to the doctor's room and said, 'Doctor, please save that tender child.' She pleaded with him humbly, with a heavy heart. But he did not even bother to have a look at the child or to do a check-up. She was greatly pained at this callous attitude.

Undeterred by this setback, Linda ran to the Nursing Supervisor and explained the matter. The hospital had all the arrangements and equipment necessary to save that tender child. But none of them raised a little finger to save a human life. And the child had the misfortune to convulse and die right next to the Oxygen mask and tube.

But Linda was shattered ever since this incident. She would still keep crying at times, saying: 'Oh! That innocent child died right before my eyes despite the availability of all arrangements to save it. And I couldn't do anything about it.'

If that child had received proper attention and care, it might have been alive today. With tears in her eyes, Linda said that the memories of that child keep haunting her to this day.

Such cold-blooded murder of little children both in the womb and outside of it has become a curse upon the modern world.

We have people who fight for life, liberty, equality, human rights, etc., and against all forms of evil. But why is it that they do not feel responsible to raise their voice against those who deny the right of innocent little children who are unable to speak or to protect themselves?

Being silent in the face of injustice is a crime against humanity.

14

A Dad for Two Rupees

S ome memories that stay ever fresh in our mind must have something special about them. They may include some mischiefs and pranks, blunders and jokes, and humorous happenings. Such are also the memories revolving around our bygone culture, heritage, and training that are engraved in our minds. Let me share some interesting episodes from the era of my childhood learning.

When I was a child, I used to go to learn letters from Kaniyan Asan in today's terms, LKG. Memories of those days keep racing into my mind: We were about twenty-five students in all, ages three and a half to five. Carrying pack lunch in hand, we had to walk about two kilometres to reach the nursery school.

At times Kaniyan Asan would come late to school. You should have seen the commotion right then—a school without a teacher! The children would create such a ruckus, yelling at each other, scratching someone with their fingernails here and there, and what not. A school without a teacher is always tumultuous. When the teacher is in, it is all calm and quiet. We all need someone to respect and obey; that will bring peace into our lives.

While this went on, someone would say: 'Hey, watch out! Asan is coming!'

As soon as he entered, all of us would spring to our feet and stand quietly with folded hands. If you had seen our posture then, you would have thought we were a bunch of innocent kids who could never ever do any mischief.

When I was reading in school, I had to walk about three kilometres from my house to reach there. But there was a short-cut that saved time and made it faster to get to school.

Therefore, our gang of students used to jump the fence with our school bags slung across our shoulders. Many days passed in this manner. One day, as usual, we reached the fence and found a man sitting on the farm with a stick in his hand. We ignored him and were about to jump the fence when he asked: 'Hey kids, where are you headed?'

'We? We are going to school,' I replied nonchalantly.

'Fine, but make sure you never again step into my farm. Find another way to go. Did you hear that?' cautioned the man, we all quietly went along the normal route.

Whenever we used to go happily along that farm and the fence, I always knew that it was not the right thing to do. But we couldn't care less, and kept on trespassing that way day after day. But once the owner declared a rule saying that we should no longer go through his land, we understood that things could go wrong if we trespassed again. After hearing his demand, I never again made an attempt to go that way.

Some things are forbidden although we may like it. We must never wilfully violate rules and laws. We should never take things that belong to another without permission. Such lessons got stamped into our heads through many incidents like the incident of one I just wrote about.

Here is another interesting experience from my school days. Some students would never tell their parents if they had been sent out of the class for doing some mischief. The only way they can get back in class was to bring his or her father to meet the teacher. Instead of bringing their own parents, they would go to the marketplace, find someone, pay him two rupees, and bring him to school as a proxy guardian.

During my eighth grade year in school, once a smart boy brought a tea shop owner as his proxy father. As bad luck would have it, the teacher had had a tea at the same tea shop sometime in the past. I guess there is no need for me to explain any further: The boy had to endure such punishment that he would never forget this in his life!

Why do some students behave so? Why do they tamper with their progress reports? Parents expect their children to be cent per cent perfect in all things. If they fall short, then they will not get the love and recognition they expect; instead there will be beatings and quarrels, and feelings of rejection. Unconditional love of parents is inevitable for stability and growing confidence in their children.

This episode also teaches us that if we try to fake, we will get caught anyway.

Occasionally, I run into my friend who had once brought his proxy father to school for two rupees. The moment I see him, I am reminded of that incident. It must be the same with him too. And that is why there was always a naughty smile on his face.

School life indeed was my textbook.

Companions, pranks, and sightseeing taught me many lessons for life. Reading, listening, sharing—there was so much to learn there too.

When I was young, my parents bought several books and kept at home for us children to read. One book that I remember vividly was the biography of a Christian Sadhu from Kerala.

The book cover has a photo of the preacher—an emaciated face with short-cropped hair, an ordinary-looking man.

His life routines, dealings, responses, the songs he penned, the circumstances that prompted him to write, the house where he lived, the surroundings—in short, all these things deeply touched my heart at a very young age. That biography which I read greatly influenced my life even without my being conscious of it.

Another book I read when I lived in North India was the biography of Sadhu Sundar Singh of Punjab (1889-1929). Once I visited the village where Sadhu Sundar

Singh was born. I visited the house wherein he had once seen Jesus Christ in a direct vision. I stood in that room and thought for a while about his life. Those experiences influenced my life tremendously.

In short, when I lived in North India for two years thereafter, I shaved my head clean, and wore a saffron-coloured dress. And people began to address me with the prefix 'Sadhu' added to my name.

In my youth, when I read the life story of Sadhu Sundar Singh, I had a desire to become like him and live like him.

When we read the biographies of other illustrious persons, their experiences, their pains and sorrows, their achievements and setbacks—all these influence our own lives too.

We must learn lessons as much from experiences as from knowledge gained through reading, travels, and conversations. It has been well said that 'experience is the teacher.'

Our entire life teaches us such little things, if only we are willing to learn.

15

Be Kind to Animals

During the severe floods in Kerala the year 2019, a Hindi-speaking friend asked me:

'Sir, your native land isn't so good; is it?'
'Why?'
'It all gets submerged under water if it rains.'
'Does that mean the land is bad?' I quipped.

Perhaps, thinking that he had made a mistake by asking me if the land was bad, he said, 'No, Sir. Isn't it very difficult if everything gets flooded? That's why asked.'

'Do you know anything about my native land?' I continued. 'Kuttanad holds the Top 2 spot in Kerala for rice production. And then, there are so many poets, writers and artists from here. Nature's beauty is beyond words.'

My friend nodded his head. Kuttanad is a land where cultural history resides. Niranam and contiguous areas are part of Kuttanad.

The Thrikkapaleeswaram temple here is an ancient landmark. The Kannassa poets lived here. St Thomas came with his missionary work first to Niranam. His port of entry has been conserved to this day.[1] Saint Geevarghese Mar Gregorios (Parumala Thirumeni) spent a good part of his life at Niranam.[2]

Kavalam Narayana Panicker who gave us the sopana (Kerala's unique genre of temple music) that imbibes the rhythms of the native unarthupattu (the 'Awakening Song'), and Thakazhi Sivasankara Pillai who presented us the idyllic life of Kuttanad with his moving stories—they are all sons of Kuttanad.[3] As I remembered all these, I thanked God that I was blessed to be born here. I also felt proud that the great-grandfather of Kadappilaril family from Pakalomattom branch moved from Kuravilangad and settled at Niranam.

Kuttanad is a land that teaches us the love of nature. It is true that floods keep drowning people's lives in misery from time to time. Nonetheless, such misery has become a matter of habit for them. They have no complaints. This earth and water combine to form the rhythm of their lives.

Thakazhi and Basheer (Vaikkom Muhammad Basheer) are two great writers that taught us to love nature and its flora and fauna. Thakazhi is Kuttanad's own novelist. And Basheer, fondly called the 'Sultan of Beypore,' is a renowned story-teller.

I was fascinated by Thakazhi's natural depiction of idyllic life and Basheer's intuitive adoption of the language of the folks.

Vellappokkathil (In the Flood), a beautiful short story written by Thakazhi, depicts the horrors of the flood:

Chennan who had been living in a thatched hut shifted to Ambalappuzha in the wake of the flood. He could not take his beloved dog along. The theme of the story revolves around the dog's body language and expressions, hopes and disappointments, and finally its tragic death. This story gives insight into the need for loving and being compassionate to animals. Thakazhi deftly drives home the point that they too have affection and sentiments.

Chennan loaded all his belongings into the boat and was all set to go. The boat moved forward. But none remembered about their dog. The dog stood there unmoving till the boat vanished from sight. It went up to the housetop growling, as though bidding Goodbye to the world.

The concluding part of this story brings tears to one's eyes:

After a long while, the dog looked in the direction that the boat went and barked vehemently.

It was now close to midnight.

After a while, the hut fell to the ground and sank into the water. Nothing was standing or visible in the endless stretch of water. That devoted dog had guarded its master's house till death. Then the house collapsed and sank. It fully sank to the bottom of the water.

The floodwater started to recede. Chennan came swimming to the hut in search of his dog. He saw a dog's carcass lying beneath a coconut tree. The waves were gently rocking it.[4]

None could have written a more moving account of the helplessness and pathetic plight of an animal trapped in a calamity. This story taught me the great truth that, just like human beings, the birds and animals on the earth also deserve to be loved.

Having finished reading the story, I was struck by more convictions. We must love not only humankind but also all living beings.

An incident that occurred in my youth comes into my mind as though it took place right here and now. There was a coconut tree in our neighbour's farm. In a cleft on its crest, some parrots with red stripes around their necks could be seen getting in and out every day.

My friend Tom and I used to look at this often with great interest. One day Tom said to me: 'Hey, Yohannan. There are baby parrots in that cleft. I will climb up and get them. You can take one of them.'

I was mad with joy. We made a thalaip (an improvised grip-stay for the feet to clamber up a tree) with a towel for my friend to climb up the tree. He struggled up, straining and lunging forward, and reached near the cleft. Tom gently put his hand into the cleft. Hurray! There were two parrot chicks! Somehow or other, Tom grabbed the chicks and came sliding down.

He gave me one parrot chick and kept the bigger one for himself. Both of us started to look after the chicks with great care. Unfortunately, my sweet little parrot chick died within two days.

But my friend Tom brought up his chick very well, feeding it with milk and a variety of fruits. He also got pecked by the parrot a number of times.

Months passed by. And the parrot began to call him by name, 'Tom . . . Tom . . .' It did not hesitate to call him 'Dog' or 'Cat' when it was angry with him.

When the parrot used to see other parrots sitting on tree branches, talking, and flying about in freedom, it would become restless and walk around in the cage. Often, it would try to cut open the cage bars with its beaks. It seemed to be always perturbed by an inexplicable restlessness.

One day, as Tom opened the doors of the cage to feed the parrot, it seized upon the opportunity and flew away. It thus achieved its life-long desire.

That was the day that made Tom saddest ever. But it was also the day of liberation for the parrot. And that is the freedom which every living being always longs for.

Birds and animals want freedom. How freely they live in the forests! We put them in cages and teach them to be obedient.

We all love the 'pets' we keep at home. We give them care and attention as we do for humankind.

But here is how an ordinary thing happened in our house:

My daughter Saramma had a rabbit at home. We had bought it at her insistence. Every day, as soon as she was back from school, she would throw her books and bag away and run to see her rabbit. She would pluck grass to feed it, sing lullabies, and carry it around.

Sadly, one day the rabbit became sick all of a sudden.

Saramma told her mother: 'Mommy, let's go to the hospital with it.'

I said: 'Dear child, people will mock at us.'

She asked: 'Why do you say that? Doesn't this rabbit have a soul? Won't it go to heaven? Please, let us go to the hospital now.'

Anyway, acceding to her demand, Gisela gave it some powdered aspirin along with water and told her that it would be fine, and not to worry. The next day, on returning from school, Saramma dashed straight to see the rabbit. But it was already dead!

Saramma started to cry at the top of her voice. Everyone came running to her. Saramma held the dead rabbit close to her chest and kept wailing and sobbing. I was greatly troubled by seeing this and tears welled up in my eyes. I was astonished that this child had loved the rabbit so deeply.

Finally, she said: 'Daddy, please bury it.' I buried it as she wanted. She continued: 'Daddy, please pray for it.' Ultimately I myself had to do the funeral rites too!

I have often been thinking about Saramma's little rabbit. My ten-year-old daughter Saramma loved that rabbit a lot. And now, there it was, dead and cold. Her tender heart was broken to bits. She was wailing for her dead rabbit.

I comforted her: 'Dear child, Daddy will get you another rabbit.'

She continued to cry, saying: 'But that won't be my rabbit.'

As you read this story, think about love. Whomever or whatever you love—be it even a simple animal—your heart will break; it will cause you pain.

In this world we live in, we must give room for others to live as well. Not only for human beings, but also for birds, animals and all.

There are lots of trees in the compound of our headquarters in Thiruvalla. From mango trees, jackfruit, sapota and cashew trees to fig, orange, and avocado trees, and herbal plants—you will find all of them there.

Rare species of birds, migratory birds, and several such 'inheritors of the earth' have settled down there. You can often hear the birds singing. Once we engaged expert ornithologists to identify and take photos of the rare birds there, and to exhibit the pictures. They were able to identify over a hundred species of birds.

We have written down the name and botanical name of all the trees and exhibited there. I have especially instructed that harvesting of fruits from those trees should be done only partially.

After all, we are not the only benefactors of nature. Those fruit-bearing trees still provide a veritable feast to those 'inheritors of the earth' that have neither title deeds nor property tax receipts but freely reside and move around in those premises. Thus they live there without being afraid of anyone.

Be gentle and kind to all the creation of the Almighty.

16

A Mother's Love

We become more aware of the value of our father and mother only when we are separated and live far away from them. Parents' love, care, correction and example help lead the children to progress and success.

Once when I went home, I found my father's chair vacant. And mother's bed was empty. I felt the very same emptiness in my heart too. Whatever we may possess, we can never buy parents with money.

When I completed my High School education, I had a desire to become a priest and to serve the community. Children who have just completed their education invariably encounter the problem of people's queries.

'What next? Are you going to college or to learn some vocational skills?' Everyone you come across will shoot these questions. They did ask me too.

I would simply reply, 'Not decided yet.' It seemed as though they were more concerned about it than us. Assume that we revealed our decision to them, and the next question would follow at once: 'If you are going to College, which one?' They were curious to know that. If we named the college we were going to, then they would readily offer their comments: 'By the way, they are always on strike there . . . At the other college, the Pass percentage is poor' and so on.

My reply would put an end to all their questions, 'Not decided yet.' But the desire to become a priest and to serve the community kept surging in my mind. And I did not share this with anyone. I knew that if I made it known, I would have to face hundreds of questions. I also feared that advice and opinions might unsettle my own decision.

Finally, I decided to share this matter with a respected person of our locality, who was rather spiritually inclined. I walked about two kilometres from our house and went to meet him.

He made me sit down and enquired about the happenings and my welfare.

I said, 'My desire is to become a priest. Besides, I like to work in villages, just like the Fathers who are helping the poor.'

He looked at me closely from head to foot. I wondered if I had uttered something wrong. In those days, I was a lean and thin little boy.

He laughed. I could not understand the meaning of his laughter. I kept staring at his face.

'Do you know how many smart boys, who wanted to become priests, are now doing some other jobs as they did not get the opportunity? To become a priest, you must have great abilities and education. Listen; try to learn some job-oriented skills.'

'Hmm,' I nodded in a low tone. 'I am going,' I said and walked back two kilometres to reach home. My mother was making some curries in the kitchen.

I thought that man's opinion was right. Maybe I was no good for such things . . . what many have desired but could not achieve. I felt very disappointed.

I told my mother about my desire to become a priest. I further informed her painfully about the person whom I had met with and shared my plan, and how he had discouraged me from such a course, saying that I was good for nothing.

Immediately, my mother said: 'Son, if God has planted such a desire in your mind, never dishearten yourself. I will pray for you.' She advised me to go ahead without any hesitation. Then she gave me the money for travelling to Bangalore for attending the training conference. Thus, I got the necessary motivation and encouragement from my mother. I packed my bags and left on my journey at once.

It was two years later that I came to know my mother used to pray daily that I should go for priestly service. Although she never told me about it, my mother kept praying to God to prepare her son for that mission.

Today, as the Metropolitan of Believers Eastern Church, I am able to touch the lives of hundreds of thousands of people by travelling across the globe and doing social renewal programmes because of my mother's one word of encouragement and long years of prayer.

In the year 1974, I was in the United States doing my studies. One day, I was suddenly informed that my father had passed away. There was no way I could reach home in time for his funeral. It would take many days of journey to arrive.

My father was buried near the Kattunilam Mar Thoma church at Niranam. I vividly remember about the day I was informed about my father's demise. I went strolling alone for many hours and kept wiping my tears frequently.

My mind was filled with thoughts concerning my father. But, what became my final consolation was the good example and lifestyle that my father gave me. My father was the epitome of integrity, dedication and diligence.

My mother left the earthly abode, aged eighty-four. In my busy life, I got very little time to sit beside my mother and talk to her freely.

In the last years of her life, I could find time only to ask her, 'How are you, Mom?' and rush away.

I did not keep aside adequate time to sit beside my mother, talk to her, nurse her, and listen to her problems. That thought kept hurting me. Today I regret the fact that I forfeited that opportunity.

I know that my mother must have wished many a time to see me. She must have asked eagerly, 'Where is he?' But there is no use in talking about it now. The window of that opportunity has since been shut forever.

The day my mother died was one that made me extremely sorrowful.

My mother passed away at 6.10 a.m. on 27 August 1990. 'I am going to my Father's House,' were her last words.

My mother was a woman who knew God and lived with deep devotion. Blessed with God's gift of six children, she taught all of them, through her own exemplary life, to love God and man. Apart from that, through her own example, she also influenced twenty-one of her grandchildren and their children.

When she was admitted to a hospital after a heart ailment, I was travelling from USA to South Korea. Immediately, I cancelled my programme and returned to my mother's side.

Ever since I could remember, our mother would get up by 4.00 a.m. at early dawn and start praying. After praying for a couple of hours, she would wake us up, saying: 'Arise and pray.' It was our daily routine every morning to sit around in a circle and read the Holy Bible and pray.

Even on the hospital bed, my mother would always keep talking about spiritual things. On the eve of her demise, as a young doctor came by to check her condition, she made him sit beside her and she talked to him about spiritual matters.

Hundreds of people who had received my mother's love and care took part in the funeral rites.

Some memories from the funeral events of my mother come racing into my mind. As the youngest in the family, it was my final privilege to cover my mother's face with a light golden-bordered gossamer piece of cloth just before the lid was to be put on to close the coffin. The moment I picked up that gossamer cloth to lay it over her face, a lightning flashed through my mind. I looked at my mother's face one more time—something seemed amiss.

My mother's ear-ring was missing. And so was the golden wedding necklace. The golden wedding ring worn on her finger was not seen. All of these had been removed. I had not thought about these things earlier.

But, at this moment when I was looking at my mother for the last time upon the earth, I noticed these things. Another thing became clear to me: The Holy Scripture that my mother always used to carry in her hand was missing. The coffin lid had already been shut. The people began to leave one by one. And we walked back to our house.

Since my father's demise in 1974, we had been looking upon my eldest brother as the head of our family. On that evening, this brother called me to his room and said, 'Aren't you leaving shortly for travels abroad? So, it's good for you to be aware about our mother's bank balance and all.'

All six of us siblings used to give our mother more than enough money and other things. I thought that there must be some good amount in the bank. My brother said, 'I went through all the accounts that Mom had jotted down. The balance would not exceed a hundred rupees.'

'What?' I exclaimed.

'That's right. The details of all the money that Mom spent have also been noted down.'

At twilight on that day, we discovered that our mother kept giving financial assistance out of her savings to charity workers, the sick, students, and such other needy people. Besides, as she had instructed, her jewellery (ear-rings, wedding necklace and ring) was sold and the money kept aside for helping people in need. I kept listening to all this silently. I was not hearing the story of a lady who was known all over the world—but the example of my own mother.

We live in an age when people even abandon the mother who gave them birth. We must never be late in recognizing our mother or father. A mother is one who patiently forgives all faults and loves her children like her own life.

When was it that you last spoke a word of love, thanks and encouragement to your mother who gave you birth, suffering a lot of pangs, who loved you more than her own life, who stood with you in joys and sorrows, who cried and suffered pains for you, who cared for you and brought you up?

Do not delay any longer . . . please don't put it off for tomorrow.

17

Geriatrics and the New Generation

Since the days of my early childhood, I was always very happy to see very old people. My high school was a few kilometres from my home. As I briskly walked to the school, lugging along my heavy school bag, I would switch to a slow pace if I came across an old man along the way. Given a chance, I would also chat with him. I found it a pleasure to learn from these old folks.

I always had some special love and affection towards aged people. The moment I saw them, I would spontaneously unfurl to full-length my dhoti that was usually folded in the middle and tucked.

Some fathers and mothers would write to me about their loneliness and sufferings. The contents of some letters sometimes break my heart.

Once an aged father wrote: 'I have become an orphan. Our children have beaten and kicked me and my wife out of the house and won't let us stay there. We are virtually on the street. How can we live? Where shall we go?' They wrote these words soaked in tears and asked for advice.

In fact, as I read that particular letter, I cried. The letter was pretty long and written by an eighty-year-old man from Ernakulam. His children were all smart and well employed, but sadly, so self-content who would not look after their parents! They considered their father and mother as a burden.

How many are such fathers and mothers that live as abandoned and unwanted by their own children! Once upon a time these now old parents lived well, but today they stay helplessly in a corner of the house or on the street! Once they faced life bravely are now curled up like a snail, unable to face their children and grandchildren!

Little children, young men and women, the middle-aged adults—they are all heading towards old age; with every day that passes, they are taking a step forward towards it. I did not mention this so that you break into a lamentation saying, 'O my God! I am advancing in age.' What we need to do is, learn as much as possible about old age, think about it, and make our lives enriched.

One day, I went into a house to meet a father. I spent some time with this man who was over eighty years of age. I asked him a few questions, and he replied. His replies made me sit up and think deeply.

I asked: 'You are now over eighty years of age. Can you please tell me what is the difference between your thoughts when you were eighteen and today? When you were young, did you think the same thoughts concerning old age as you do now?'

He replied immediately:

'When I was eighteen, I thought I was a very smart guy who could do anything. In a manner of speaking, even today I think I can still do something useful, but no one seems to accept that. And they don't need my help either. So, I now tend to think that perhaps I have no competence, and I am just a nobody. Often, the thought overwhelms me that my opinions fail to carry any weight or value for the young people. And that thought leads me to dejection at times. But my intense desire is that, instead of being despondent, I must make my old age useful for others. I have a great yearning for it.

However, in the eyes of the new generation, my thoughts seem worthless and contemptible. To tell you frankly, in my youthful days, I never thought that many of my abilities would quickly pass away. Although I feel disappointed initially when I don't get acceptance from others, as I keep reflecting over it, I realize that I was at an age when I didn't think that, unlike my own self, my thoughts would also keep changing. And things are not moving these days as I then used to think they would.

Times have changed. True, I feel disappointed when others don't take my advice, for I know I have journeyed way ahead of them and gained a lot of wisdom to live a more meaningful life. Several things that I consider essential for a quality living are viewed as unnecessary for this now.' And that becomes unbearable for me.

The rich life experience of older generation is important. All of us are on this life journey and if only we are willing to learn from those that went before us.

A great hiatus or difference has come between the new generation and the geriatrics. Being unable to talk or relate to each other, or to appreciate their sentiments, the young generation and the old generation have gone far distant from each other. They exist in isolation, as though separated like night and day.

It is healthy thoughts to think to oneself, the rocking chair, the walking cane that the aged used to aid them walk, the spittoon that they keep beside their bed spit their phlegm into, the cramps and muscle-pulls that they now suffer will not spare them when they get old. Oils, herbal lotions, and a helping hand will all become indispensable requirements. The young and bright also be afflicted by old age and a greying hairline . . .

This changeover does not end here. Although time changes, it will keep travelling forward from generation to generation. Handing over the baton will keep happening over and over. Let us not forget that. There is an old saying in Malayalam that translates thus: 'The green leaf of the jackfruit tree laughs when the ripe yellow leaf falls.' We can't remain the same forever. We are all rapidly travelling towards old age. Therefore, it behooves us to examine our own attitude towards our old and fragile of our society.

Even if a person has become aged or reached a ripe old age, the value of that life never diminishes. They have only grown in age. So, young people should learn to accept the old, and to love them. Even if it demands your time, listen carefully to the words of the geriatrics. And cultivate patience in your minds.

Spend some quality time with the aged. Listen to what they tell you, and accept them because old age is life's most important portion of God's grace, and not as helpless dying people. In order that your life may become enriched so long as you live, you must selflessly love those who have reached old age and respect them.

Someone once said: 'A man's life is like a day. Childhood is the dawn of this day; youth its noon and old age its evening. Even as evening is a part of day, old age is a part of life.'

Those who remember this principle and live in accordance with it are intelligent. He who lives thinking that life as present will be always so. One day, when he reaches old age with his teeth fallen, skin wrinkled, his hair grey, and unable to walk, he will think: 'Alas! How time has flown! And I have become old.' That is the time when he will realize that life is passing, and the world's pleasures are momentary.

If a house has a grandfather or grandmother who lives with the fear of God, they will become a blessing for all the people in their surroundings.

The Holy Scripture repeatedly instructs us to respect the elderly. In many families, people do not see a grandfather or grandmother as a crown of glory, but rather as a crown of thorns—they see them as necessary evil, something to manage or put up with.

It is said, when people get older, they usually become more tender, kind and loving. But in some cases, when some people get older, they become harsh, stubborn, demanding and make the life of their children miserable. The joint family system that reflected the beauty of our Bharat culture is being eroded by the independent spirit of the Western culture and young people don't like to live with their parents, once they are married.

As I said before, unfortunately, one of the reasons for the children's behaviour has to do with the lack of love and kindness on the part of the ageing parents.

Sometime back I heard the confession from a young mother of her suffering due to the harsh treatment of her aged mother-in-law. The story she narrated revolved around her life of oppression under the overbearing authority of this aged grandmother.

She said: 'I lived there for about ten years. Once, my eldest son fell ill. The doctor prescribed kashayam (a brew) which I prepared. But the grandmother did not allow me to give the child this potion. She poured rice water into it. As a result, my son's illness became aggravated.

'Later, at a time when I had little children to look after, just when I was about to go to bed after dinner, the grandmother would measure out a large bushel of paddy and give me to de-husk. I had to de-husk the whole quantity and then pound it to powder with a pestle

and mortar, then fry the rice powder, moist it and make
puttu (a rice delicacy for breakfast) by steaming it by early
morning. The grandmother's command was to spread
a banana leaf over a mat and then lay the cooked puttu
upon it. And I had to prepare one large potful of coffee
to go with it.

'I had to work throughout the night to pound the raw
paddy, then powder the rice, and so on. Meanwhile, my
little child would wake up, hold on to the pillar, and go on
crying. The mother and children would all be sleeping like
a log. When my child cried, I would also cry along with
it and somehow spend the night till daybreak. And that's
how I managed to produce the puttu by early morning.
In short, that grandmother never ever gave me any sort of
peace or freedom.'

I felt very sad and perturbed as I heard her story.
Obviously, all fathers and mothers can't be behaving in
such a heartless and cruel manner to their daughters-in-
law.

Pause and think of what your daughter-in-law, son, or
grandchildren will be saying about you. If they get some
time to share their sentiments, what do you think they will
be talking about you? Remember how you treated them,
and then you will understand what they will be saying
about you.

Recently, I read about a little episode that actually took
place outside of India:

At a busy junction in a town, the policeman on duty
was standing in a corner near the street light. He noticed a

poor woman squatting in a corner and bending to pick up something from the ground.

The policeman suspected that she was probably picking up something valuable that had fallen from someone's hands. He approached her and asked, 'Woman, what are you doing here?'

The woman became rather restive at once.

The policeman became still more suspicious. Something was wrong! Immediately, he seized the woman's carry-bag and looked into it. It was filled with glass pieces. The policemen questioned her.

She said: 'Sir, look. The children turn around here while going to school. If these glass pieces lie scattered here, they might pierce the feet of the little kids. That's dangerous. So, I picked them all up and put them into my bag. Now I will go and throw them far away.'

The policeman was amazed. Without saying a word, he handed her the bag and walked away. This aged woman, rather frail in health, did a good deed for the sake of those children according to her ability. They must not suffer pain!

This is what we must do in our lives. Let us remove the dangerous glass pieces and all the obstacles lying in their path so that they don't get hurt or wounded, or suffer some pain; or to lighten or remove their burden. Perhaps, none may come forward to encourage us in our activity. On the other hand, some people may look at us with suspicion. Nonetheless, we must never be wearied of doing good.

Old age must become an example and a school for life's lessons to the new generation. The upcoming generation needs to rouse themselves to honour and obey the old generation.

While you can, honour and help the aged, for you too one day be in their shoes.

18

Lesson from Dabba

Once I went on a long journey along with my friend. As we were returning, it was 1.30 a.m. We stopped by a thattukada (dabba-streetside food shop) and bought some food. We had no choice, as we were returning late in the night after a meeting, and hotels were closed by then.

That night, I talked to the eatery owner for a while. He had left his native land many years ago and arrived at that town. He first worked in a hotel, cleaning tables, washing dishes, and so on. Then he joined with the chefs and learned how to cook dishes. Soon, he became a master chef. He had neither parents nor siblings.

Years passed by. He told the hotel owner: 'Sir, I will do all my work here most faithfully. But I have one request: Please give me some cash in advance.' The generous owner replied: 'No problem. I will give you the money you want.'

With the money he got from the hotel owner, he bought some materials and utensils. Once he was done with his work at the hotel, he would reach the street by night and run his thattukada. He would sleep only for four hours. Within four years, he earned as much money as he wanted! He got married and built a nice house. He has up to five workers in his thattukada. But he still keeps working at that hotel. He achieved success in his life. He accomplished things that he had never dreamed of in his life. And now, he has plans to buy a car.

A little orphan boy who was wandering in the streets, who came to clean tables at a hotel, achieved such stunning progress through sheer hard work! He was able to save all his earnings as he had no bad habits of any kind. Through unflagging diligence, he became a wealthy man!

Diligence and perseverance can give us success. But sloth and laziness will drive us to poverty. In whichever field of work we are engaged, we will never have to look for shortcuts to progress if only we have perseverance and a desire to succeed.

The daily newspapers contain several advertisements announcing job vacancies. There is a story about a man who applied for a job after seeing an advertisement. At first sight, he was a smart guy—fit, healthy, and most suitable for this job in all respects. The degrees he earned, and the special course certificates he had . . ., he seemed to be a topper all in all. He went for the interview. Before inviting him to the interview, the owners of the establishment, having carefully examined his credentials, thought that among thousands of applicants, he was the most deserving candidate. But unfortunately, he did not land the job when the interview was done. The one who appeared to be less than half suitable finally got the job.

How did this come about? All said and done, he was smart to look at, and in many other respects. But his conversations and his own self-perception were not quite healthy. His thoughts concerning his own self were such as to evoke doubts.

The moment he opened his mouth to speak, he would only talk of failures. He was unable to demonstrate himself as better and more competent than others.

In America, there is a well-known airline company, I flew with them several times. When many other air carriers were moving towards financial collapse, this company was raking in a lot of profits. Their growth graph was shooting up dramatically. I happened to read an article about it. And what was the secret behind their success? The way they select their employees—pilots, and other staff working in the airplanes—as explained by the company CEO is very interesting.

If the company gives an advertisement announcing job vacancies, they get hundreds of applications. The degrees and credentials of the applicants stay in the files. During the interview, they do not first look at their degrees or work experience. Instead, as they keep talking to each candidate, they will look into their eyes and observe their facial expressions, style of talking, their self-esteem, boldness, cheerfulness and ability to respond with humour.

The amazing secret behind their success in getting more passengers is that they have staff who are able to deal with people lovingly with a cheerful face and pleasing manners. The company hires only this type of employees. They hit upon this formula after studying the behaviour of candidates based on their outlook and disposition.

We want to be successful, get a good job, lead a nice family life, bring up our children well, and build up sound relationships in every walk of life. All these are requirements in life. But the magic key to this is neither circumstances nor other people. Instead, it is our own image of self-esteem within us that leads us to success. How do you perceive yourself? What is your outlook about your own self? Your answers will actually give you a clue as to who you are.

There are many people who cannot achieve anything in life, but live in despair without getting a job despite their best efforts and with a sense of failure, regret, and chagrin. The primary reason behind their plight is that they are unable to have a positive attitude in life.

'Oh! I am no good . . . I am quite useless . . . You mean that job? No, I can't take up that job; I don't have the competence for that!' These words reflect their own self-perception and they end up in an awful atmosphere of despondency. Eventually, they become such individuals even in the eyes of beholders.

You can never achieve success beyond the pale of your own outlook and appraisal about yourself. So, how can you gain a good appreciation about your own self?

Henry Ford (1863-1947), a world-renowned automobile manufacturer, began his life in a powerhouse for a meagre salary of Rs 150. Born in an ordinary family in the year 1863, Ford went to school till he reached fifteen years of age. Endowed with unusual talent and brilliant ideas, Ford made amazing progress rapidly. Ford, who made billions of automobile vehicles, bearing his own name and popular throughout the world, began his life in a humble way.

No one is born great. We have the power to make our own personality magnetic and dynamic.

How can we build up a healthy outlook and a sound personality perspective in an individual? Is that determined by that person's house, car, estate, education, wealth; or by body structure, shape of the nose, colour of hair, skin complexion; or by others' opinion about him/her; or by such other things? Certainly not.

What does Psychology say about it? It is nothing but what lies in a person's mind, his own feelings about self in the invisible world, his own opinion about himself, the value that he assigns to himself. That emotion speaks to him thus: 'I like me, I don't hate me' or 'I don't like me.' These are expressions of self-image. To put it differently, your self-image is the picture you draw of yourself.

An individual's unique disposition is called 'personality.' It is the sum total of one's habits, behaviour, and character.

A job applicant might look like a prince or princess. They have all the degrees and credentials on paper. But, when they talk face to face, they do not get the job. Why does this happen? Although everything else is in place, it is their own self-image, self-perception and outlook that actually determine their future.

These days, there are scores of institutions that give training on how to appear for job interviews. If you pay them Rs 5,000 or Rs 10,000, they will train you within a week or four-five days. They will train you in every way, such as, how to sit at the interview; how to rest your arms; how to be dressed; how to answer questions; the tone of your voice when you reply, and so on.

Just for the time when a man has to attend an interview, they will train him and teach him how to express his personality for that purpose. In reality, he may not possess that personality. But he will pretend or simulate. He may get the job if he is lucky. But, in the long run, his real personality will emerge from within. As his own self-image is narrow and distorted, he might even lose his job. Or he will simply stagnate without any progress in life.

The quality of our life depends on the way we talk, behave, and respond in life depend upon the manner in which we think about ourselves. This has been proved beyond doubt by psychologists. In other words, the normal behaviour of individuals and their actions are always closely related to the way they think about themselves inwardly.

A man may be an imbecile or ignorant idiot, and his own perception about himself may be the worst possible. Nonetheless, there may come a time when he suddenly performs a stunning feat, even as the sun comes rising and shining after a great storm with thunder, rains and dark clouds has abated. Or he may achieve some special success. However, before long, he will revert to his original condition, just like the proverbial dog's tail that is inserted into a pipe to straighten it.

When we pull a rubber band, it keeps stretching both ways. But, the moment we release it, it regains its original position. The lives of many people are similar to this. Their lives keep bobbing up and down without being steady.

If we read, understand, and believe in, the teachings contained in the Holy Scriptures, our mind and our emotions will get transformed. And if that happens, our behaviour and actions will also be aligned in accordance with them.

Assume that we donate Rs 1,00,000 to a beggar. His condition and lifestyle will not improve with that. How often have we been reading in newspapers about beggars who die by the wayside with five, six, ten or twenty lakhs of rupees in cash kept in their pockets or baggage!

Recently, I read in the local daily about such a man. Although a beggar, he possesses hundreds of thousands of rupees. He has bank deposits, and has lent money to several people. But he begs on the streets—that is to say, he sees himself as a beggar.

We have a native dialogue on these lines: 'Hey, look at him. He was born into a royal family . . . Though he doesn't have wealth or a glittering suit to put on, yet his demeanour and dealings truly declare his identity.' His personality does not consist of wealth or degrees, but instead, he is inwardly conscious as to who he is. And he behaves accordingly.

We must make it a habit to be aware of our own capabilities and accept our own worth. I do not go after what others say about me. I am convinced that if we can formulate a philosophy of life that makes us do the right things, then success is assured. There is no doubt that the street food shop owner I met has motivated me to be ever diligent and persevering.

There is no shortcut to success other than hard work and persistence.

19

What You Are: Appearance and Reality

When I was studying in college in America, once I went along with some friends to visit an Art Gallery. Along one flank of the large hall in a massive building, the portraits of world-renowned artists such as Michelangelo, Picasso, and Leonardo Da Vinci were exhibited. I remember those portraits even to this day.

Imagine that we are going to another art exhibition now. We have entered through the wide doors lying open before us. In front of the hall hangs a board with the words 'The Touch of the Guru.' On either side of the hall, dozens of paintings elegantly framed have been displayed on the walls. Who was the artist that conceived these lively-looking pictures beautifully captured in stunning colours? We keep admiring each picture in wonder! We feel as though they are talking to us. What could be the message they are conveying to us?

Our attention now focuses on one painting: Here sits a potter, and a wheel keeps turning in front of him. Above it is a heap of dirt! At the bottom of this painting is written: 'The worthless dirt.'

Next to it hangs another painting. The same potter is seen there as well. But now he is holding not the useless mud in his hands, but instead an exquisitely crafted pot. That 'worthless dirt' has been transformed into a strikingly beautiful pot after getting the potter's touch and going through the deft caresses of his fingers. The label at its bottom reads, 'The priceless dirt.'

Following this analogy, how does your personality get formed? In other words, how do you get the awareness as to who you are?

I happened to read 'The Seven Habits of Highly Effective People' by Stephen Covey sometime back. He has written therein about a problem that we all commonly face—the question of our self-identity. Who am I? What is my personality? He argues that our personality is moulded through the reality of 'Social Mirror.'[1]

What does this mean? It means that from the time a child is born, it keeps observing as in a mirror what others say about it—father, mother, siblings, uncles and aunts, or friends, neighbours, teachers, and so on. There is always a mirror in front of this child, this youth. What it keeps reflecting is others' opinions and comments about them. By repeatedly hearing what others say about them, they become aware of what they are.

I look back to the days when I was learning about the mirror during my Science class at school. We learned about concave mirrors, convex mirrors, etc. If we look into a mirror with its surface caved in, how will our face appear? It will look totally distorted and misshapen. But, if we look into a normal mirror, we will see our real image.

If you take your mirror and smash it with a hammer to shatter the glass in pieces, and then look into the same mirror, how will your face appear in it? Certainly not your real face, but rather it will reflect a face that is cut into pieces and apparently wounded. Assume that the glass pieces have fallen down. In that case, nothing will be visible. Our personality development occurs in the same manner.

We do not realize the fact that what others are saying about us most of the time do not make up our real picture. A father and mother keep telling a young girl: 'Oh! You don't have a brain! And your appearance! Who will look at you? You will never get anyone to marry you . . .' By repeatedly saying such things, they are actually fostering a negative self-image in her mind. Actually, she does not think of herself as God sees her and thinks about her; instead, she thinks as others think about her. She will expect things to happen in her life according to the perspectives and self-image in her mind about herself.

Let us assume that a marriage proposal has come up for this girl. She can only hope and pray that the proposal will go through positively, because the perspective she got so far has always been adverse and on the line of, 'Who will come forward to marry me?' She does not know where she got such a perspective. The negative self-image and deprecatory thoughts lying within her subconscious mind keep reflecting on her face, conversation, and decisions.

Often, others' opinions and 'social mirror' are not the only factors that play a role in the personality development of people. The experiences—good and bad—that individuals face in their life also help mould their personalities and perspectives.

I am often pained by the caste system that still prevails in our country. I doubt whether there is any such retrograde and despicable system worse than this anywhere in the world. Millions of people live like slaves in this country, owing to their differences in caste. I lived in North India for eight years. You will be shocked to hear this: At some places, if a low-caste man or woman unwittingly touches the body of an upper-caste person or draws water from the latter's well, they will be punished for it. You may find it hard to believe, but that is the reality. I have seen with my own eyes the dark side of the caste system—the immense sufferings and hardship of the people.[2]

What would a man born in a low caste family be telling himself? 'However much I try, can I ever get any progress here? No, I can't get any better. I was born into this caste.' But I firmly believe in a God who loves everyone regardless of caste or creed. My dear friend, God does not look at your colour, caste, or clan. Aren't you a human being? Then God surely loves you.

Consider this scenario: A millionaire born in an upper-caste family is admitted to a hospital for a critical illness. He is at the point of death. If he is not given a blood transfusion urgently, he will be gone forever. People are running around desperately for a blood donor. But the required blood group is not available anywhere. Finally, they come upon a scavenger—one born in the lowest caste and living on the street, with neither kith nor kin. His blood group is a perfect match. Will this upper-caste patient then protest, saying, 'No. No, I don't want his blood?' Rather, he will insist that the entire blood of the donor be taken, because he wants to live. But, when he was in the prime of health, if the poor scavenger happened to touch any part of his body by chance, they would have beaten him to death.

Pause and think: What a dark and dismal situation we are facing today! If you were born in a poor, low caste family, and by tradition you do not have a degree, position, or dignity, then you should never think of establishing your personality or personal worth upon any of those factors. But instead, your real worth, who you are must be based on the Creator God who is the God of all people regardless of caste, creed, religion, language or nationality. We must see ourselves as God's children and precious to Him.

Also, never forget, no one can hurt you with their words, attitude and actions unless you allow them. You have the freedom of choice to reject or receive what others dish out to you.

Your attitude to what happens to you determines your future.

20

Choose for Yourself: Positive Thinking

Sometime ago, I happened to read a story about three trees from a children's book of tales. It was an imaginative story. An olive tree, an oak tree, and a pine tree—these three trees were growing on a mountain slope. They became very tall and big. As they were growing, they kept sharing their dreams with one another, even as children talk among themselves.

The olive tree said: 'One day, I will become a casket that is used to keep valuable jewellery and the costliest pearls. I will be kept honourably in the inner treasury of a palace. I will be most securely guarded.' But, do you know what actually happened? As time passed, this olive tree was cut down. Finally, it became part of a stable for cattle. The olive tree was in great distress, thinking, 'This is not what I dreamed of becoming. See what has happened to me!'

The oak tree desired to become a large ship one day. And the world's most famous kings and thinkers would travel by this ship. But as time passed, it was cut down and became a fisherman's small boat—a little boat filled with stinking, rotten fishes, wet fishing nets, etc. The oak tree was in great distress, thinking, 'Alas! See my plight. This is not what I dreamed of becoming!'

The pine tree was next. Standing on the mountain slope, it had grown tall and big, almost touching the sky. One day, massive lightning struck and split the tree in two, and it fell. It was cut into pieces of logs and kept in a godown. Years passed by . . .

One day, in a stable, in the company of cattle, a little child was born. It was that olive tree that sheltered the child. After several years, Jesus of Nazareth sat on that stinking fishing boat and began teaching about the Kingdom of God. The oak tree then realized what a great fortune he had come by.

After about three years, Christ was being crucified upon a tree with three nails to bring healing and reconciliation to mankind with their God. As the Roman soldiers went in search of a suitable tree for this purpose, they came across the logs of that pine tree. They used those logs to make the cross.

Although this is an imaginary tale, it contains some food for thought. Very often, we think just as these three trees thought. We want to come up in life, hold our heads high before everyone; others should recognize our achievements, and so on. But, look at my plight now! My dreams, desires, opportunities, interests, and all have come to nothing. My life has not progressed according to my plans. I did not get a job; my marriage has not happened; I did not get the good fortunes I hoped for—such are our complaints before God. However, do not forget the fact that God has a much better plan for you.

When I was young, I heard a story as follows: An astrologer was walking along the bank of a river. He had an umbrella in hand. It was not an umbrella commonly used, but one made of palm leaf. As he was walking along, he saw a ferocious dog chained in front of a house on the opposite bank. He said to himself: 'O my God! If this river dries up, that dog will break the chain and come running to bite me.' Obsessed with this terrifying thought, he tore his umbrella and held its handle in his hand to use as a stick. And he stood on the bank, waiting for the dog to come rushing at him!

While this is not an actual incident, we can learn a good lesson from it. Our thoughts and expectations greatly influence our lives. And that is why the Holy Scripture says that a man becomes as he thinks.

If your thoughts are always negative, and you see only problems in your life, then you can never expect success in life. Mahatma Gandhi once said: 'A man is but the product of his thoughts. What he thinks, he becomes.'[1]

Let me share an experience. This happened many years ago. A man used to work in our office. In the early days, I used to ask his opinion before starting anything new or launching a new programme or project. But whenever I broached the subject, he would immediately pick out its negative aspects. Unknowingly, this used to weary my mind and make me discouraged.

As a result, I became less and less interested in taking up a new venture or doing something new. One day, as I thought about this in-depth, I realized one thing—that my contact with that person was harmful to me. Whenever I talked to him about such things, his reply would never be 'Certainly, we can manage that,' or 'No problem; there's a way we can do it.' Repeatedly hearing the negative aspects of such things, my mind became restive and my courage seemed to be draining away from me. So, finally I decided to refrain from sharing any of my thoughts or plans with that person. I altogether avoided my conversations with him. Thus, I made a great escape.

Believe it or not, our future is decided by the present. The influences we allow into our lives, if they are from the negative people, they will damage our thinking and our wrong, negative thinking will result in damaging our possibilities.

The Holy Scripture says, as we think our thoughts, so our lives will become. Thoughts are powerful. They create either hope, health, well-being or the opposite.

Your mind is the battleground. Think positive thoughts as a way of life.

The expression 'worried to death' has more truth to it than you might think.

There is a story about Nick Sitzman, a strong, young bull-of-a-man, who worked on a train crew. It seemed

Nick had everything: a strong healthy body, ambition, a wife and two children, and many friends. However, Nick had one fault. He was a notorious worrier. He worried about everything and usually feared the worst.[2]

One midsummer day, the train crew were informed that they could quit an hour early in honour of the foreman's birthday. Accidentally, Nick was locked in a refrigerator boxcar, and the rest of the workmen left the site. Nick panicked.

He banged and shouted until his fists were bloody and his voice was hoarse. No one heard him. 'If I can't get out, I'll freeze to death in here,' he thought. Wanting to let his wife and family know exactly what had happened to him, Nick found a knife and began to etch words on the wooden floor. He wrote, 'It's so cold, my body is getting numb. If I could just go to sleep. These may be my last words.'

The next morning the crew slid open the heavy doors of the boxcar and found Nick dead. An autopsy revealed that every physical sign of his body indicated he had frozen to death. And yet the refrigeration unit of the car was inoperative, and the temperature inside indicated fifty-five degrees. Nick had killed himself by the power of negative thinking.

Can someone really think himself to death? That is the point of this legend: the mind is a powerful thing; so powerful that it can kill. This story has often been passed along by motivational speakers as an example of the power of one's mind.

We've been hearing versions of this story for years, tales in which the details change but the theme remains that of an unfortunate man who dies after he is trapped in a situation which he presumes to be dangerous but is later revealed not to have posed any real threat to his well-being: The air-tight room he's locked in turns out to have a vent to the outside which brings a steady supply of fresh air but the man suffocates because he believes he's used up all the oxygen; the cooling unit on the refrigerated boxcar he's trapped in isn't turned on, but the man stuck inside the car slowly succumbs to hypothermia nonetheless.

Because this type of story involves a death caused by something contradictory to the physical evidence, a search of the deceased's pockets or a quick glance at the floor or walls will inevitably turn up a note detailing the final hours of his life. The note is a necessary plot element in this sort of tale, as the victim's thoughts just prior to his death are key to the story, and those are details we couldn't know without his conveniently having left a written record of what he'd been thinking.

The theme of a physically unharmed victim who passes away only because he believes himself to be dying underpins another urban legend. In 'Lethal Indirection,' a fellow who believes himself to have been executed dies of a heart attack.

Could someone really think himself to death? The jury may still be out on that concept, but we've yet to find any documentation for the claim that someone once died because his power of thought turned him into a corpsicle.

Our thoughts and expectations have tremendous influence over us. They will either make or mar our life; make it better or damned.

Choose for yourself.

21

I Hate My Husband!

When I was a child, I was very fond of balloons. I used to spend all my pocket money to buy balloons. When I was reading in Grade Four or Five, a peddler with balloons came near our school and began to sell.

The balloons I saw with him were larger than any I had seen in my life. When he blew air into it, some of them would grow big and stretch very long, while others would become large and round like footballs. He would blow them into such huge shapes that it seemed amazing and hard to believe. But the price of one such balloon was equal to that of twenty normal balloons!

I decided to buy one at whatever cost. From the money I got from my mother, I managed to buy one the following day. Many students did likewise.

Huh! We would fill our lungs, hold our breath, and blow the balloon so hard that it would swell as big as an elephant, covering our face, shoulder and hands! Problems and predicaments in our life are similar to this. When you take a problem into your hands and keep blowing into it, it will grow so big as to hide your face from seeing anything else. There is a saying 'for the tree miss the forest.'

In other words, when I blow into a balloon and inflate it, can I see anything that lies behind it? No, I can see nothing beyond the blown-up balloon in front of my eyes! Instead of looking only at problems, we should be able to see their solutions and possibilities for them. We need to have a forward-looking vision. A mind that is sound enough to see beyond problems is indispensable to ensure success in our endeavours.

I happened to read a true story about a village in Africa. At a low-lying land in this village, a group of people suddenly began to fall ill. Their skin would break out into eruptions, the flesh would suppurate, and finally they would die. It seemed to be some kind of a viral infection. Soon enough, the concerned government officials learned about it and sent an expert Medical Team to investigate this breakout. This peculiar incidence was confined to that village. Finally, they tested the water at that locality and found it to be contaminated with traces of a particular poisonous substance. But they had no clue whatsoever as to its source.

Ultimately they extended their search and reached the source of the river from which the villagers got their water. There, they found a number of dead pigs lying decomposed! No one had seen them. They were tangled in the river. The bacteria formed from the remains of those decomposed pigs had caused many of those villagers to fall ill and die. They got rid of them and thus found a solution to end the problem.[1]

As I was reading this story, my thoughts were on these lines: How many families are living with their hearts and minds in great darkness, their homes immersed in a stressful and turbulent environment, with quarrels and cursing, although they do not die due to bodily illness or festers! Individuals living together are unable to say one word of love to one another. They have large palace-like mansions with expensive equipment and installations. But disquiet reigns over their house. If anyone there opens one's mouth to speak, only words of swearing, curses, and cussedness come out. They are actually dying. Why? What's the problem?

Instead of a river of life and peace flowing from their hearts, it is poison that comes forth. And why does that happen? Because, even as it happened in the African village, the source of that river is sullied with putrefied things. People who live with hatred and vengeance, unable to forgive others, carry hearts that are contaminated with the roots of bitterness. So, what comes out of them are sordid things that harm, hurt and kill fellow beings.

If we carry a handful of fiery cinder in our palm to throw at a neighbour, won't our palm get burned? If we try to throw muck at another, won't our hands get smeared in muck? And if it is cow dung, won't it be the same? When we do such things, apart from others' lives, our own lives also get sullied.

To have our mind and body in full bloom of health is an indispensable part of a joyful and peaceful life. But, more often than not, most people are unable to achieve this.

Let me tell you a true story based on the experiences of a psychiatrist.

A woman who intensely hated her husband came to him for treatment. The first words she spoke were: 'I hate my husband.'

The psychiatrist asked: 'What has he done, that you hate him so much?'

'He hasn't done anything, but I hate him. I can't live with him,' she said.

After weeks of counselling, the truth came out. When she was young, she went to have a bath, and three boys raped her. Then she screamed and shouted: 'I hate men. They are all devils.' These were her words of bitterness and hatred. 'I will never allow a man to touch my body,' she shouted in anger. Those words of hatred fell deep into her heart. And so, she had been living all her life in hatred.

As time passed, she got married. However, the seed that fell deep into her heart sprouted and became a tree. Now, she was reaping its fruit. She never let go of the things she had to forget. But, after receiving expert counselling from doctors and psychiatrists, by God's grace, her life became enriched and happy because, she forgave those who hurt her from the bottom of her heart. Why did she do that? Not for the transgressors' good, but for herself, as she badly needed healing. We can never get healed by wreaking vengeance.

This is how we should pray: 'Lord, I don't know several things that lie hidden within my heart, and keep hurting and paining me, and smothering the goodness in me. So, please give me awareness. Lord, please examine my heart and reveal to me those problems that cause me sorrow and regret, loss and downfall, disease and disquiet, loneliness and turbulence. Please lead me to walk in the steady path of peace, love and kindness.'

There are times when I retreat all by myself to a quiet corner—such as the foot of a tree, the cover of a culvert, in a room, by the wayside, or beside the ferry point that juts into a river—to look into my heart. If we can forget and forgive others for the things they have done to us in the days gone by, and willingly decide to live, giving up that bitterness and animosity, then our mind will gain mental health and happiness.

At Niranam, where I was born and brought up, people don't use monkeys to climb up a coconut tree and pluck coconuts. Nor do they use a makeshift bamboo ladder to climb up. I have heard that such things are done in Malaysia. But here, we have men who climb up the tree all by themselves. They will climb up the tall coconut tree and cut down bunches of coconuts from the dizzying height. An onlooker on the ground will freeze with fear if he looks up. A climber can cut down coconut bunches from fifty to 100 trees in a day. But, if he has fractured his leg or his body is diseased and festering, will he be able to climb up a tree? Never. A coconut tree climber needs very strong arms. If he does not hold on to the tree firmly even as a monkey sits on the branch of a tree, he will fall flat on the ground with a great thud. He will die on the spot. So, it is absolutely essential that a climber has very strong legs and arms.

A sick man cannot climb up a coconut tree. If he stands at the foot of the tree and commands, 'Hey, coconuts! Come down here,' they will not obey. In the same way, those who want to achieve progress, success, and blessings in life must understand this truth: Although it is good for a person to desire for such things as 'I must gain a deep spiritual life,' or 'I must achieve greater heights in material prosperity,' or 'My children should have a bright future,' they can become a reality only if that person has good health—not of body, but mind.

The invisible walls that you build to keep others away, out of bitterness and hatred, actually do not serve to keep others away from you, but instead you are only building a prison cell for yourself. A wife may think that their conjugal problem will go away if she sleeps alone in a separate room, or if she avoids close contact with him. The husband may think likewise, and so can children think the same. But what actually happens is that, in the process, they are only tearing themselves apart in pieces.

Our duty is to forget and forgive from the bottom of our heart. And God will do the rest for us. If we can understand this truth, our lives will become meaningful and enriched.

Forgiveness is the best remedy to heal our broken hearts.

22

In Search of Faithfulness

Don't we all like sincere and faithful people? Recently I read about a woman who selflessly did a good deed.

In the northern tip of Scotland there is a cluster of islands called Orkney Islands. On the seashore lived a family that did fishing for their livelihood. Once when the man was returning after fishing, he lost his way at sea. In those days there were no lighthouses or other sources of light to indicate land to seafarers. Finally, as his boat floundered and sank, the man died. His little daughter was deeply distressed at her father's death. She resolved to do everything in her means to ensure that in future fishermen do not meet with such a tragic end as her father. From that day, she made her day into night, and night into day. Every day at dusk she would light a candle and keep it at the window of their small house; then she would take a bundle of cotton and spin it into yarn while she took care to see that the candlelight did not dim. It thus became her habit to sleep only during the day. She used part of the money she earned through spinning to buy candles.

In this manner, for about fifty years, her loving service prevented many ships and boats from getting shattered on the rocks nearby. Perhaps, thousands of seafarers travelling by ships across that treacherous sea by night would have seen that little light at a distance and thanked God for it.[1]

Our lives should be such that they give light to others. A candle flame should burn within us so that it safeguards their lives from getting destroyed in the darkness. People hate those who are double-faced. I know one such man.

He was an aristocrat whom people held in high regard. In his youth, when he was in High School, he was elected as the student leader. At college he was a political activist and leader.

He made steady progress step by step. Eventually, he became a top leader in the political party. He could eloquently deliver speeches non-stop for up to three hours. No one would get bored listening to him.

Anyone could easily fall into his magic spell. People jostled to gather around him, even as ants would rush in large numbers towards a pot of honey. Gradually, over sixty lower rung leaders started to work under him as regular party workers. It was his nature to deal lovingly with anyone who approached him. His words were as sweet as honey. When he passed by, people would exclaim: 'Oh! What a gem of a man! Political leaders should be like him.'

When Chackochan and friends met him, he listened to them attentively. The secret behind their reinforced faith in the leader was evident in these words: 'If he had not loved us or cared for us, he would never have shared with us the confidential matters concerning Mathunni and his secret conspiracy against us. Surely, he has so much concern for us.'

Mathunni arrived the very same evening. When Chackochan and his gang had come at early dawn, they were let into all the secret things concerning Mathunni. And now, Mathunni has come with his men. The leader talked to them in detail for about four hours.

As they were on their way back, they said: 'This guy is really with us. He listened to all our problems and promised to do everything possible. Moreover, he has told us all the confidential things concerning Chackochan. Actually, he is a man who loves us. Come hell or high water, he will always stand by us firmly.'

After a few years, this leader's closest friends and admirers began to walk away from him one after the other. An unexplained rancour against him began to grow in their hearts. He kept on flattering people and revealing others' secrets simply to please them. He pretended to be the intimate friend of anyone who approached him.

As years passed by, the circle came round in full. Everyone had realized by now that this man was talking about everyone in the very same fashion. He would never speak well about anyone. Any secret matter shared with him was sure to become public before long. This man could never be trusted!

There is always a warning sign 'DANGER' before an electrical installation. People began to run away from him just like a man who flees from danger out of fear, or like a driver who manoeuvres his vehicle away from a pothole, or like children who run for their life on sighting a dog. What happened finally? He became a lonely man, shunned by one and all.

Let me share another story. The most vital competence a person must have in order to succeed in life and to achieve things is trustworthiness. But it is a sad fact that most people do not know its value.

Assume that you are an unmarried girl. Marriage proposal has come for you to marry a man in the nearby town. His name is 'Earthworm' Skaria.

Here is how he describes about the merits of a suitable boy he has identified for you: 'He is from a traditional, pedigree family. His father is a well-known aristocrat in the locality. The boy is his only son. There are no other claimants to his property. As for education, the boy has passed school and college with high ranks. Tall and well built, fair like a foreigner, smart and healthy, and a frontrunner in politics. If things go well, there is a good chance of his becoming a Minister . . .'

After hearing all this, your father quips: 'Hey, from what you have said, it looks like this boy has come from the moon!'

'No, Uncle. He has a small weakness, though,' replies Skaria.

'And what's that?'

'Oh! I heard that he has been having a little affair with two or three girls. And they say that two of them have borne him children. I did enquire about it and found it to be true. That's the small little fault he has.'

Let me ask you: Will your parents and family members let this 'Earthworm' Skaria go scot-free? Howsoever wealthy and smart a boy might be, no girl will ever want to marry a man who has such a character. No father who loves his daughter will ever agree to such an alliance because, this boy is not faithful, but a deceiver.

And the girl will say that she will prefer to marry a beggar and sleep on the street rather than accept such a brute as husband. Why? Simply because, although he has everything, he is not faithful.

We can always find people who are compassionate, kind, loving, and charitable towards others. But how hard it is to find a faithful man! People look for faithful people as they search for treasure. Be it at home, locality, school, hospital, or anywhere else, people are in search of a faithful person.

When we are considering a marriage proposal, we enquire with our acquaintances all around. How was the boy since his school days? How was the girl during her studies and stay at the hostel? What kind of a person is he? How is her character?

Let me ask a few questions to make you think:

Will you vote for a politician who is a turncoat?
Will you trust a priest who leaks your secrets?

Will you approach a grocer who sells rice adulterated with soil?

Will anyone hire a taxi or auto-rickshaw that levies exorbitant fare?

Will you engage a lazy labourer who sits idle without doing work?

Will you lend a second loan to a man who has failed to return the previous loan promptly?

Will you sincerely trust in, and share your closest secrets with, a person who gossips about you?

Will anyone trust a person who leaves mid-way?

Will you wait for a man who has never been punctual?

Will you again visit a petrol pump that adulterates fuel?

Will you trust and befriend a man who lives with an attitude of earning a penny by hook or crook?

Will you trust a man who only utters lies when he opens his mouth?

Will you trust a person who does not keep his word?

Will you trust a man who wants to survive even by stamping down another?

Will you retain an employee who is untrustworthy?

Will anyone trust a person who goes around and spreads gossip and calumny about the company and its owners, and leaks its secrets?

Will you always entertain a self-conceited person who lives with high ego, pretending that he knows everything?

Would you wish to help a person who has never expressed a word of gratitude for several favours that you have already done?

The answer to all the above questions is an emphatic 'NO'.

Imagine that you are the boss of a company. You have invited some candidates for recruiting into your firm. About a hundred applicants have turned up for the interview. One of the candidates tells you: 'I have a PhD in this subject. I am smart and very competent. I am fit and in good health.' He has handed over all his certificates in support. As part of the hiring process, you do the background check on the potential employee from the reference he gave on the previous places of his employment. And with all the qualities this young man has, you learn he is a gossiper who reveals confidential information to others.

What will you do with this smart guy? Obviously, you will not hire him.

Then comes another candidate. He is not so smart or fighting fit. But he is well-behaved and gentle, with average education. He is dedicated to his work, and says, 'If I get this job, I will be faithful to the company and bosses, and sincerely work for you to the best of my abilities.' And you do the same diligence to check this man's character etc. and learn what he said about himself is more than true.

Out of these two, whom will you select? A company or bank will always look for such a person who is faithful and trustworthy.

What is the worst crime that a citizen can do against one's own country? That is to betray one's motherland to enemies, pass on secret information, and engage in spying. How does that country deal with such traitors who engage in espionage? It will wipe them out from the face of this earth.

One morning, the newspaper headlines ran a story about a man whom the people held in high esteem: He was working as a traitor and has been nabbed for that crime. Whatever good things he did for the people in the past will be of no account now, because he was not faithful. He did not possess a good character.

All over the world, people are earnestly seeking after trustworthy people. In his bestseller, 'Seven Habits of Effective people', Steven R. Covey talks about the most important element of any truly successful people is 'TRUST'—character is more important than abilities.

If the tree is good, the fruit will be good.

23

Keep This Secret

A man once said that building a good life and forming a good character are both like cultivating teak.

Once I went along with some friends to visit a place in Tamil Nadu, called Tenkasi. I had another friend at that place. As we were travelling by his jeep, we saw a teak plantation. He pulled his jeep to the side and, pointing at the trees standing there, said: 'Look, those are all teak trees.'

I was shocked and asked him: 'How can that be? Teak? They are all pencil-thin and standing crooked.'

I always thought that teak was a straight and thick tree that grows tall like a coconut tree.

He laughed and replied: 'This guy bought over a hundred acres of land and planted a large number of teak saplings. He never looked back. If you plant a teak sapling, you must fasten it to a straight backstop and prune its branches. You must care for it like little children if you want it to grow into a good and shapely tree.'

Our character formation is similar to this. A day or month or year is not enough to become a person whom others love, accept, and respect. Developing a good character is a slightly harder process. Nonetheless, it is certainly achievable if only we try.

A man named Frank is one of my most intimate friends. I first met him in Bangalore in 1967. He was the Head of a Charity organization in those days.

Once, Frank worked in a high position in Mumbai. He has a wife and three children. He resigned his job, sold his house and belongings, and joined the Charity Organization to help the poor and needy.

He is smart and educated. But the point here is not salary, education, talents, competencies, commitment, sacrifice, or any such thing, because these are qualities that many others also possess.

There is one special thing that stands out in Frank. I am not the only one to say that, but everyone who knows him say the same thing, that howsoever heavily depressed, after talking to Frank, within a few minutes, they find hope and confidence.

What is the secret behind this? He never criticizes anyone. He cries with those who cry. He helps those in need. Even if it causes him hurt or damage, he will never disclose secrets.

He never talks bad about people. Some would jokingly comment that Frank could never talk ill even of Satan, instead he will say, one thing for sure, the devil is hard working. Frank spends all his time and abilities for others day and night. However much a person is fallen, he never rejects them, but instead binds up their wounds and comforts them.

He is a man who loves others and wants to do good in everything he does. But if anyone does something wrong, he points out the mistake lovingly, saying: 'Look, This is not right.'

Let me share an unforgettable experience: One of my friends once asked me about a man whom I knew, 'How is he? I'll keep it a closely guarded secret. I'll never share it with anyone.'

My habit was to generally speak only about the good things concerning another person. However, as this enquiry was rather serious in nature and its consequences might adversely impact many others, I agreed to reveal certain things. But I requested them to ensure that what I shared was strictly kept confidential. I did not tell them, though, that in the light of my disclosures, they should not act against him or that they should refrain from doing it for him.

At first, I enumerated all his good qualities. Thereafter, I also shared a couple of his weaknesses that I personally knew.

What happened next was the proverbial case of the remedy being worse than the disease. About two days after the closure of this enquiry, the target came rushing at me like a seasoned and venomous cobra. I asked him at once: 'Hey, What's the matter?' He snapped: 'Matter? Are you kidding and making a fool of me? I know what all things you told them about me. I never thought you were such a man!'

Finally I told him: 'Are you done with what you had to say? Aren't the things I told them about you cent per cent correct? Didn't they happen exactly as such?'

He replied angrily: 'Whether it happened or not isn't the question. But I never ever thought you would do it to me.'

How did all this come about? The problem began when I revealed to them some information about this man on the condition that they would never disclose it. And what did they do? As soon as they met him, they directly let the cat out of the bag, saying, 'Hey, you know, we asked so-and-so about you, and he told us such-and-such things.' How grievous a heartburn and misunderstanding their indiscretion caused him and me!

I know pretty well that you would have suffered such wounds, or even deeper ones, on more than one occasion. Maybe, you are currently experiencing it. That has happened as the person with whom you shared a secret in good faith and strict confidence has broadcasted it in the marketplace. A person who does such things is not at all faithful or trustworthy.

This happened long ago: When Sujatha was in college, she fell in love with a boy. She went to college by bus. She would talk with him for a while when they met; nothing more. After about sixteen years, she got married, and had two children. Rajan was the boy who had studied with her, back then.

Whenever Rajan used to come across Sujatha's husband, his stomach would have a restless feeling. Why did that happen? He wanted to tell Sujatha's husband about their friendship, but finally blurted out these words: 'Hey, your wife and I studied together in . . . college. In those days she had some company. He and I were friends . . .' Telling things as they were truly would not sound interesting. So, he added some spice to his narration and served it with some exaggeration, half-truths, and untruths.

Think about it. If you are one that gossiper doing the talebearing, what do you gain from this? How would it benefit you? Will you get happiness from others' pain, sorrow, family breakdown, and suicide?

Even by superficial introspection, you may uncover the many failures of your past such as not speaking the whole truth, taking bribes, being cruel to your family members, unfaithful in money matters and hurting others with unloving attitude and actions. Failures never need to determine your future. Learn from it and accept God's love and mercy. This is the way of blessing.

Let me ask you a straightforward question: if you honestly disclose all the things you know about yourself, what will people think of you? No one wish to live as an ostracized person. We don't want people to hate us. If that be so, let us remember the words of Christ, 'Do unto others what you wish others do for you.'[1] In other words, do not do bad to others that you wish others do to you.

There is nothing more important than loyalty for a lifelong friendship. True love buries a mountain of faults.

24

Worthy of Love: The Way to Work

Once I was talking to a man. He was the owner of a company with over sixty workers. He started to narrate an incident.

His company was in need of a couple of new employees. The posts were advertised and a large number of people applied. Interviews were arranged for some shortlisted candidates.

He continued: 'There was a smart guy among them. He was a six-foot-tall and very handsome man. He had earned many high-level degrees from the university, and seemed exceptionally capable.

The owner thought that he might never get a more suitable candidate. However, he entrusted another expert to have a conversation with him. The expert found out an interesting fact in the process—that the candidate had worked for seven employers at different locations in the last seven years, and had never had a tenure exceeding one year at any of these companies. He further explored as to why this happened and found the reasons very interesting.

Wherever he worked, his sole objective was to gain experience there and then land a better job elsewhere. He would spend all his time for his own progress without showing any faithfulness or commitment to his present establishment. And he would keep wasting his work hours by chatting over the phone with several people. That was the character of this smart candidate.

They did not hire him for the job. No doubt, he was smart, competent, fit and healthy. But he lacked sincerity. He was like a rolling stone, with neither stability nor steadfastness.

Be it in a company, hospital, establishment, workplace, or wherever else, we must work with gratitude in our hearts. Besides, we must act with commitment and faithfulness towards the superiors that God has appointed over us.

Opportunists are on the increase these days. These self-centered folks' attitude is, 'I must get what I want even if it takes to knock off someone else. Everything should go well with me even if the establishment goes to dogs.' Such a person will get knocked out in the long run. He will never be able to get blessings or experience goodness. What we need today more than ever before are not smart and competent people, but trustworthy people.

The Holy Scripture narrates an incident that occurred long before Christ was born. A family consisting of husband, wife, and two sons lived in Bethlehem, community in the country of Israel. In those days, people were in great misery due to a severe famine; even bedbugs starved to death.

One day, the parents discussed this matter with their children: 'We are in great trouble. What shall we do?' Finally they decided to leave their homeland and go to a neighbouring country.

Unlike modern times, there was no need for a passport or Visa in those days. They departed from their home and started their journey to the foreign land. They arrived at a place called Moab, an ancient Kingdom that is today located in modern state of Jordan. They planned to return to their homeland after a few months when the famine would end.

We know that many people from their native land go to other foreign lands to eke out a living, and live there happily. In the same manner, this family also went there with great hopes. All their desires were fulfilled, and they had no problem of livelihood whatsoever.

As time passed, their plans had to be revised. Both their sons wanted to get married. Instead of returning to their homeland, they married two Moabite girls.

In the first place, it was God's commandment that they should never depart from their own homeland. If they went out of their community, they would give up their identity and culture.

They were aware of all the consequence. But they went there for a short time to escape from starvation and death. However, finally the sons entered into marriage relationship with the people of different faith and culture.

Years passed by rapidly. It was the tenth year when some misfortunes started to visit that family. The woman's husband died, and soon after, both her sons passed away. Now, only the woman Naomi and her two young daughters-in-law remained. Three widows in the house! Can you imagine the depths of their great sorrow and solitude? And the disdain they faced must have been immense.

The story does not end here. Meanwhile, news came that the famine in Bethlehem, Naomi's homeland, had ended. Food and water was available in plenty. 'Why don't we return to Bethlehem?' thought Naomi seriously.

Wherever we travel across the globe, we invariably carry along some unforgettable memories of our own homeland, such as the boiled jackfruit dish, tapioca, Dal fry, coconut chutney, sambar, Idli, Puri-pani, Samosa and curd curry, and so on. Similarly, Naomi nursed some such memories in her heart.

Naomi called both daughters-in-law and told them: 'Dear children: Moab, where you were born and grew up, is your own homeland and country. Your parents, relations, friends, kith and kin, and acquaintances are all here. You can live here. Let me go back alone to my homeland.'

The girls' names were Orpah and Ruth.

Both these women were deeply troubled when they heard the words of the mother-in-law. Finally, Orpah decided to return to her folks. She cried bitterly. She hugged and kissed her mother-in-law, and then returned to her own home.

But Ruth told Naomi: 'Mom, I won't go.'

Naomi replied: 'Look, Orpah is gone. So, please go on as she did.'

Ruth said: 'Mom, please don't say that. Don't ask me to return to my folks. I will go with you wherever you go. And I will live where you live. Your God will be my God, and your people my people. I will die where you die. I will not leave you under any circumstances.'[1]

Even as little monkeys cling to the breasts of their mother, Ruth stuck on to Naomi.

The story continues. Both of them started on their journey. From early morning, they covered a good distance, braving the blazing sun and the dust. Naomi walked with the help of a stick, and finally they reached Bethlehem.

Here is an old woman. She has neither a house nor children, not even an address. She has lost everything. The name 'Naomi' means 'delight' or 'pleasantness' and so on. But, in this situation, she changed her name to 'Mara,' meaning 'filled with bitterness.'

Let us ask Ruth a few questions: 'Hi, Ruth, you set out along with this aged mother-in-law. What did you gain by doing that? You are young and healthy. Your folks and friends, parents and uncles, and all are in Moab. You have a bright future if only you live there. But instead, if you go along with Naomi, you know they are totally different from your people. They will treat you as an outcast.

Ruth's reply: 'My future, my safety, and my welfare are not my main concern. I love my Mom. Her husband and sons died. Having reached old age, she is now an orphan.

Her children died . . . So, I will look after Mom. I will live for Mom. And I will die where Mom dies.'

Think about it. This is love. And this is faithfulness.

We are living in a world filled with lazy, self-centred people. There are some offices where hundreds of people work. But they will not complete the work that requires only one day to complete even after months. They will keep sipping tea, chatting and gossiping, and idle away their time. Or they go out for a break now and then. And at the end, they will get their salaries dishonestly without rendering the work.

There are such endless stories happening in our land. The people are sighing and lamenting with heavy hearts because of this situation. Today, one can get nothing done without paying bribes—no matter where you go.

Why do such things happen? Employees without commitment and dedication, those who are not faithful to the nation, and are lazy to the core—they keep earning salaries without working. Their attitude is 'No matter who suffers, or how many people are pressed into starvation, that is none of my concern. I must have my way!'

A few years ago, a man wrote me a lengthy letter about crisis they are in and request for prayer. He was working in a good position in North India, with a fat pay package. His wife and children were residing in his native place.

Meanwhile, someone told him that if he returned to his homeland and started a business, he could make much more money and his future more secure. He believed it and invested huge sum he had in bank to start a business.

One of his close friends at his native place joined as a partner. So, they launched their business. They would travel together, eat together, and think together: such thick friends that it seemed they would die together and be buried in the same grave!

Time went by, and their business grew way beyond their expectations. They had high earnings and many employees in office.

After some years, their thriving business began to run into losses gradually. The reason was none other than manipulation of accounts and cash. Here is what happened:

The friend and partner who had invested not a lot into this business was very smart and shrewd. He manipulated and forged signatures and financial documents. In short, the business finally came into his hands. The one who had resigned his job and invested massive amount had lost all. He was broken-hearted and in deep despair. And now he stays home under treatment for his mental breakdown. And his former partner, now runs the business as if he is the owner of the business and everything associated with it.

People who behave in this manner are a dime a dozen these days. He steps into his job by kowtowing and grovelling before the boss, calling him, 'Sir' and 'Lord' and all. When he enters into his job, he is so exemplary in work and obedience that it would seem there is none as well-behaved as he the world over.

But hold on! In a year or two, his colour would change, much like a chameleon. When he joined, he had no moustache, but now he sports terrific whiskers. When he first came to the job, he would stand deferentially with folded hands, but now he does not even bother to rise up from his chair when the boss approaches him. Now his postures and attitude seem to shout out, 'Who the hell is this guy?' It is indeed hard to believe that this is the same guy who had first signed up for the job!

This has been happening in many an establishment. Company owners distressed for this reason are galore. Employees who become unfaithful as time passes are numerous. Once they are able to stand on their own feet, having learned the tricks of the trade, they start kicking their own mentors. They conveniently forget the past, ignore the present situation, forsake their commitment and affiliation, and chart a course of their own.

On the other hand, a trustworthy person will never do that. People who are worthy of love will always display belongingness and faithfulness. Although they are capable of doing things themselves, they will always be subordinate to their boss.

A boy has been working with us for over a year and a half. Someone approached him and said: 'I will get you a 'first-class' job. You will earn double the salary you get here. You will have a bright future there.'

He replied: 'If I leave and join there, I may get more money and a better future. But what I am doing here is much more important. So many people who are facing problems, pain, and sorrow keep writing to us, asking for help and advice. God has appointed me here so that we can send them words of comfort and solace. I will not give up this job.'

Loyalty is more important than ability.

25

The Gains behind the Pains

In the year 1968, I lived in Ajmer in Rajasthan. After six months of life in Rajasthan, I suffered a bout of jaundice, and I was admitted in the Government hospital in Ajmer.

I had neither relatives nor acquaintances in Rajasthan. At the hospital where I was being treated, several patients were accommodated in one room. I occupied one of the beds. I was disheartened to know that there was none to speak a comforting word of love to me, to care for me, or talk to me in my native lingo. All the brethren stood around me and prayed, and then they left, saying that God would take care of me. I nodded in agreement. And I lay there with a weary heart, tired, sad and hopeless.

After a few hours, a nurse came and asked me: 'Where are you from?'

I replied, 'Kerala.'

Immediately she started talking to me in Malayalam. What a relief! I felt. Hearing that, I felt as though my illness had reduced by half. This fifty-year-old woman lovingly talked to me, age seventeen, as she would talk to her own son. She was great a help with all necessary arrangements to give me medicines and food etc.

Whenever I think about a hospital and its staff, my memory from Ajmer Rajasthan comes to my mind. God showed me mercy by assigning that loving nurse to give me comfort and encouragement as I lay there hopeless and alone.

When a crisis occurs, nature always has a solution in store for it. I have often felt that the sorrows we face in life are actually stepping stones to happiness.

One of my friends lives abroad. One day, when he was out of station, a situation arose such that his wife had to drive the car alone for shopping and she was seven months pregnant.

As she was driving, another vehicle crashed head-on into her car. It was a terrible accident. However, by God's grace, she escaped without sustaining any injury. She didn't know how she escaped unhurt. But her car was completely crushed in that collision. Many people came running and gathered around the spot; so did policemen. Finally, she took a taxi and reached home.

Her husband came home in the evening. She feared that her husband would scold her for having destroyed their car through the collision. As soon as she saw her husband, she became restless and began to fret. Her expression changed, and she became highly emotional. Her husband asked: 'What's the matter with you?' She said hesitantly, 'Promise me that you won't scold me.' He replied: 'No, I won't scold you. Let me know what's the matter.'

Then she said, 'Around noon today, when I was driving, another car came crashing into our car. It got crushed like a pappadam (a thin, crisp, round flatbread). I alone survived.' He was shocked on hearing this.

Instantly, he told her: 'I don't care if that car, or any number of cars, gets destroyed. Thank God you are not hurt. God was merciful to us.'

It is praiseworthy that this husband was able to look at material losses with composure and value human life. In some cases of loss or critical situations, we need to stay calm and pray for God's help. Our conscience and common sense will also guide us if we stay calm and not panic.

There is a book titled Apollo-13. It presents the story of the men who undertook space travel to the moon. Midway through the travel, the oxygen tank burst. Beneath their capsule in outer space, the temperature was below Minus twenty-eight—in other words, extremely cold! Their Oxygen supply would run out within a few hours. Any which way they looked at, it seemed virtually impossible for them to return to earth.

At the same time, the scientists at NASA in Houston were running around frantically, not knowing what to do. Just then, the astronauts attentively heard the voice of the Chief Scientist coming from the Control Room loud and clear: 'Friends, don't be afraid at all. You can return to earth without any difficulty. Simply follow my instructions meticulously, and everything will be fine. We know what's your problem . . . We can fix it.' Thus, he gave them some directions, and they followed it verbatim. Therefore, they did not lose their life, but were able to return to earth without any difficulty.[1]

When we become powerless, we only need to obey— our conscience, Nature, God, an Invisible Power . . .

Let me share an incident which reminds us that we are denied some things in life only for our good.

As the priest of their church read Psalm 19, verses 1-2 at church, describing the splendours in space, the little boy Frank Blazek kept listening in wonder. Whether sleeping or at lunch, Frank's mind was always obsessed with the dream that he should travel through space.

Born to ordinary parents in a village, Frank knew that it was a pipe dream that no common man could ever hope to achieve. Nonetheless, Frank earned his degree with Science as an optional subject, and later became a Science Teacher.

Meanwhile, the U.S. Government decided to include a common citizen as a crew member of the Space Shuttle. President Ronald Reagan made an announcement concerning this. It was decided that a common teacher should be selected for the Shuttle journey. Over 11,000 teachers across the United States applied for the selection. Out of them, a hundred men and women were shortlisted and sent to the NASA training centre. Frank was one among this hundred.

As he was going through his training at the Space Centre, Frank thought that his dream was being fulfilled. Frank's family, student companions, and his church kept constantly praying and fasting for him. With great hopes, Frank returned home after completing his training. He believed that he would certainly get the opportunity to travel in space.

However, NASA finally selected another teacher, Christa McAuliffe. On hearing this news, Frank was literally devastated. He even doubted the efficacy of prayers and God. He was shattered by his utter disappointment and sorrow in failing to realize the dream that he had been fondly nursing since childhood. But Frank's father was a firm warrior of faith. He held the grieving Frank close and told him: 'Nothing happens without a reason. It's always for our good, and not for our harm.' But Frank did not find solace in this either.

On 28 January 1986 the space shuttle Challenger shot off into space, carrying seven crew members. Christa McAuliffe was one among them. Within a few minutes from its launch, Challenger exploded in the sky, resulting in the death of all seven crew members including Christa. As he watched this tragic event unfolding on the television, Frank remembered his father's morale-boosting words. The disaster that Challenger suffered helped open Frank's eyes. He learned to look at life's disappointments in the light of God's care and plans for us.[2]

Please don't misunderstand, I am not saying God cared for Frank and He didn't care for Christa. Life is full of mysteries, all we can do is to accept what we live with and have the unknown to the Almighty God.

When our hopes are dashed, or when faced with painful and saddening experiences, we naturally tend to become disheartened. But we should never consider them as a loss, as there is always a lot of goodness and gains that come with it.

I happened to read a little book titled 'Don't Waste Your Sorrows' a few days back. If someone tells you, 'Hey, please don't waste your success, your achievement, or the millions that you just earned,' it certainly makes sense. But instead, if you are told to not waste your pains and sorrows, your sighs and tears, and your wants, will you be able to digest and appreciate that? In order to understand that, you must have a vision that sees things as God sees them.

One of the disciples of Christ, St Peter is said to have often reminded his hearers not to be surprised if they find themselves at the centre of a stormy ordeal. What he says here is that when trials and tribulations come, we must not take them too seriously. This is means for God to bless us.

A person who is blessed with good health, happiness, success, progress and a favourable situation may be able to tell his suffering neighbour thus: 'Friend, don't worry. These are minor things. They will pass away. Cheer up!' The value of his words are far less compared to a man who suffered much and came through it all can say to a suffering family or friend to hold on, don't give up.

When we are dealing with problems, it is important to keep in mind that people are not your enemy. Your wife is not your enemy. Your husband is not your enemy. Your children are not your enemy. But rather, these adverse circumstances and pressures are piling up over you so that rivers of life and goodness may break forth from within you.

Never give up.

26

The Human Touch: A Smile
Also Matters

When we hear about success, progress, prosperity, a bright future, and so on, we tend to think that it refers to some things we gain which we do not possess. But in fact, the secret behind real progress or living a blessed life does not consist in possessing material things, but rather in giving.

If we keep looking only at ourselves constantly, we will become blind before long. In other words, our eyes of joy become so stone-blind that we are unable to see, accept or experience goodness and blessings in life.

A true story comes to my mind. In the shady part of a large city, many illiterate, poor and alcohol-addicted people lived. Wealthy and successful people would never reside in that part of the city. Some priests and nuns of the Catholic

Church started a school in that neighbourhood. Their objective was not to attract the children of the affluent, but rather to help the abandoned and orphan children who were wandering in the streets. These well-educated and capable priests and Sisters were spending their time and energy for this purpose.

Hundreds of destitute children started to study in this school. What a joyful sight it was to see those little children coming, smartly dressed in uniforms and carrying their school bags! This made a huge difference in the community at large.

Gradually, more and more destitute children flocked to the school, so much so that there was no space in the small school building to accommodate them. The school authorities were in a dilemma, not knowing what to do.

Several buildings and plots around the school were available for sale. But the Sisters and priests had no money to buy them. So, they began to pray.

In the meantime, they learned that many acres of land and buildings adjoining the school belonged to a seventy-five-year-old businessman. They enquired further and came to know that the owner was one of the biggest misers in the locality. They wished to get that property free of cost, but they knew that asking a favour from a miser was like trying to make a hole in water.

Nevertheless, finally they approached this man. He mocked and ridiculed them when they made their request known. They left, dejected and disappointed. After a week, this miser suffered a sudden heart attack. People gathered around him and shifted him to a hospital. As he lay there for treatment, an unexpected transformation occurred in his life. The priests and Sisters visited him at the hospital.

To make the long story short, this miser began to tell himself: 'Ugh! After all, I have grown so old. And I own property worth crores of rupees. But, when I suffered the heart attack, if I had not gotten this slightest chance to survive and instead died, all my wealth and property would have gone to someone else for their enjoyment. So, why am I amassing all these?'

He realized that he was an unhappy man living in utter solitude, shunned by society and disliked by one and all. Even beggars would not come to his gates because they had already spread the news in the neighbourhood, saying, 'Don't ever go near that gate. That miser won't give a paisa. Instead he will let loose his dog upon you.'

Finally, his own emptiness flashed upon his mind. Then he called those priests and Sisters and asked them: 'Don't you want this plot and building?'

They could not believe their ears. They replied: 'But we have no money to pay you.'

For the first time, they saw a terrific smile on his face. He continued: 'Here's the key. It belongs to you. You don't have to pay me a single paisa. It's only now that, in my entire life, I've been able to smile for the first time, to sleep soundly without sleeping pills, to look at and enjoy Nature, birds and the street, to be joyful, to hum a tune, and walk around.'

You may be a millionaire or the owner of an estate, an ordinary school teacher or a fisherman, an auto-rickshaw driver or an office clerk. Whatever your position in life, it is not your material possessions that give happiness, peace, and prosperity in your life. But rather, your decision to personally open up your heart and love others and to help others with large-hearted generosity lies behind all that.

When you come across others who are in dire need, don't walk away from them. Instead, utilise your time and money to recognize their pain and empathize with them, to visit patients at the hospital by squeezing your scarce time, and to help the poorest of the poor.

You are the richest person if you have the betterment of others' lives as your life's goal. Then you will be the owner of a truly blessed life. It took the businessman a heart-attack in order to understand this truth.

You and I have received a short life span to spend upon the face of this earth. During this tenure, we are fortunate if only we can remember the words that Jesus Christ spoke, 'to love your neighbour as yourself'[1] and, without focusing on our own selfish interests, we are able to see others' pain, sorrows, wants, tears and sighs, and give them a helping hand.

Christ taught us, 'Give and you shall receive.'[2] If we are able to perceive others' needs and sufferings and accordingly love them, care for them, give to them, and strengthen them, then we will become truly blessed. This is a secret that we must internalise.

Many people generally think about what they can get or snatch and hoard, and they imagine that thereby they can become rich, wealthy, successful and happy.

On the other hand, if you love others from the bottom of your heart and give generously to them, then you will progress in every field. When we say 'give' most people think about giving monetary assistance.

There are so many things we can give that cannot be bought for money and are invaluable. How valuable it is if you can simply look at a person and smile! That smile expresses the fact that you recognize them and acknowledge their presence. What is required is merely a look of recognition, love, care, and sympathy.

Your son or daughter does not need a bicycle, a bike or Rs 1,00,000. No, what you can give them, and is much more valuable, is just a loving embrace, and some words of acceptance, love, affection, and care.

What you can give that person is not money; but beyond that, a word filled with love, or a comforting caress. Yes, what they expect is your love and kindness.

At times, the people around you may need some financial help. If you are able, please help them. That is love in action.

When does our pet dog at home wag its tail? When you come home after work, your presence, your look, and your calling out its name—these become a trigger for your dog, which loves you and you love, to wag its tail.

If that is so, the people we deal with and talk to, and those who live with us at home also need a look of compassion and concern.

Let me share with you a touching experience: A woman delivered twins at a hospital—one male and the other female. But the doctors observed that the girl child had some physical problem. On detailed examination, they diagnosed that the baby's heart had some problem, and she was struggling to breathe. Everyone was worried. As it was a premature delivery, both babies were kept in two separate incubators.

After a few days, the girl child's health condition began to deteriorate. A nurse who had several years of experience there told the doctor: 'Doctor, I have a suggestion. We have now kept these two babies in separate incubators. Let us put both of them into one incubator and that may make a difference.'

The doctor replied: 'What do you mean? Of what use will that be?'

'Doctor, please give it a chance,' the nurse pleaded.

Finally, although it was against medical convention, the doctor agreed. The nurse laid both babies in one incubator. Now both were lying together as they did in the mother's womb. After a few hours, the healthy boy child placed one of his hands upon his sister whose health was worsening. The doctor and the nurse were witnessing this wonderful scene. Within a few days the health of the girl child that was on the verge of death dramatically improved. Later on, both these twins grew up into healthy children, studied together, and became successful in life. This is a true life story.

A loving embrace, a caress, a touch of hand—even if our human intelligence or our tradition cannot comprehend this, we have no choice but to believe in it.

Those living in the prison cell of solitude with sorrows and mental tension, those living like animals with their heads bent under a yoke and unable to raise their heads due to sharply lacerating words, chatter, and gossip from others—such persons are all around us.

Those who are hungry; street wanderers and destitutes; beggars, and poverty-stricken children bearing life's burden at a tender age of five, six or seven, unable to buy a pencil, pen and notebook for going to school; children carrying bricks, stones and cement; poor, emaciated and under-nourished women with suckling babies breaking stones with a hammer by the wayside for livelihood—how many are such people living in misery all around us!

Why do we keep things at home that we don't regularly use? We have so many saris, blouses, trousers, and shirts stacked away in the cupboard, but we won't give them away to some needy persons and do not mind if they are eaten up by cockroaches or moths. Our children are grown up and in college; their dresses will no longer suit them. Still, we never think of donating them to someone. Finally, when they are too old, worn out, and unfit for use, we try to give them away to somebody. Those rags become worthless!

In any case, our life on earth is restricted to fifty, sixty, or seventy years. When you die, your beloved son and grandchildren will not send your watch, gold ring or anything along with you. You will go empty-handed just as you came. Therefore, so long as you live, do some good deeds for those who are living in poverty, hunger, pain, and sorrow. Let their laughter and happiness become your life's joy, contentment and blessing.

Love is a feeling to be experienced by loving hugs and warm handshake.

27

Gratitude

It is a good habit to say 'Thank You.' It is a sign of gentleness and good upbringing.

When we help someone that involves some sacrifice on our part, we naturally expect a word of thanks from them. And if they don't, our heart rankles a little with a feeling of suffocation.

I remember an incident that happened when I spent some years in Rajasthan. It was a day in the summer. The sun was blazing hot! It was so warm that a bucket of water kept in the sun would start boiling.

We were travelling to a place by train. We were in the Third Class compartment, then nicknamed 'Gandhi Class' (this class has since been abolished). This bogie was jam-packed with passengers, most of them Marwaris (traders). Along with them were chicken, ducks, animals, gunny bags, bundles, and what not! In short, there was hardly room to stand. Add to these the sweltering heat and sweat—altogether an unbearable situation! Luckily, I got a seat and squeezed myself into it.

Just then I found an old lady standing in front of me. She was so advanced in age that I thought she might collapse any moment and die. Seeing her pathetic condition, I stood up and vacated my seat for her. But what surprised me was that, let alone a word of thanks like 'God bless you, child,' there was not even the slightest sign of gratitude on her face.

In North India, normally people say 'Dhanyavaad,' meaning 'Thank You' whenever you do something for them.

I thought to myself: 'O God, although I did such a favour to her, she did not utter a word of thanks, even by way of a glance. How ungrateful people are!'

Only a selfless mind can say 'Thank You.' We cannot assign a value to the word 'Thanks.' But I learned one thing: When we do a favour, we must never expect anything in return from them. Even to this day, I follow that principle.

One little boy came up to his mother in the kitchen one evening while she was fixing supper, and he handed her a piece of paper that he had been writing on. After his mom dried her hands on an apron, she read it, and this is what it said:

For cutting the grass	$5.00
For cleaning up my room this week	$1.00
For going to the store for you	$.50
Baby-sitting my kid brother while you went shopping	$.25
Taking out the garbage	$1.00
For getting a good report card	$5.00
For cleaning up and raking the yard	$2.00
Total owed:	$14.75

Well, I'll tell you, his mother looked at him standing there expectantly, and boy, could I see the memories flashing through her mind. So she picked up the pen, turned over the paper he'd written on, and this is what she wrote:

For the nine months I carried you while you were growing inside me, No Charge.

For all the nights that I've sat up with you, doctored and prayed for you, No Charge.

For all the trying times, and all the tears that you've caused through the years, there's No Charge.

When you add it all up, the cost of my love is No Charge.

For all the nights that were filled with dread, and for the worries I knew were ahead, No Charge.

For the toys, food, clothes, and even wiping your nose, there's No Charge, Son.

> And when you add it all up, the full cost of real love
> is No Charge.

Well, friends, when our son finished reading what his mother had written, there were great big old tears in his eyes, and he looked straight up at his mother and said, 'Mom, I sure do love you.' And then he took the pen and in great big letters he wrote: 'PAID IN FULL.'[1]

I lived in North India for many years. A phrase that people regularly use there in their conversation is 'Bhai Saheb, Dhanyawaad,' meaning 'Thanks sir.' Those who speak in Urdu would say 'Shukriya.'

Once, a smart boy wrote me a letter. It contained a piece of criticism against me: 'Sir, why should we always keep saying "Thanks"? Are you trying to teach us something new?'

Generally, this is a word that is rarely used in some cultures. I keep wondering if 'Thanks' is still a word that seems unwieldy for our tongue to pronounce.

An episode from the pages of history goes like this: One story I heard from the life of Akbar, who appreciated music so much. Akbar the Great was an emperor who appreciated music. Once, the world-renowned Hindustani classical vocalist Tansen rendered mellifluous and captivating songs with this exceptional voice and talent. The audience in the court was left speechless with the magic of his beautiful songs.

The emperor rewarded Tansen with many gifts and said: 'O great singer, your singing has been most wonderful.

I doubt if there is anyone else in the whole world who can sing so well.'

Tansen immediately replied: Your Highness, please don't praise me thus. The songs of my guru Haridas are so much better than mine. I believe Your Highness has never heard him singing.'

At the emperor's command, Haridas came to his palace a few days later. He rendered an exceptionally mesmerizing song at the emperor's court. The emperor and the audience in the court got immersed in that celestial strain of music.

The emperor ordered to give precious and invaluable gifts to Haridas. But the latter most humbly declined to accept any. Then Akbar the Great asked Tansen: 'Tansen, why can't you sing like Haridas?'

Tansen replied: 'Your Highness, I am singing to please men. But my guru sings to please God.'[2]

This vocalist could have told the emperor that there was none in the world capable of singing better than me. But instead, he humbled himself and acted as one grateful to his guru.

Similarly, we should always be grateful to others and to God. An ungrateful heart will always be filled with pride.

Pause. Take time to think and reflect upon the many good things that have happened to you in the life journey— you will be surprised and overwhelmed by the blessings and good fortunes you have enjoyed. Look up and say, 'God thank You,' and too, develop the habit to say, 'Thank you' to others.

28

The Tomb with the Light of Faithfulness

One day, as I was walking by our parish church, my eyes fell upon the cemetery. The church had a stone wall running all around it. I peered over it and found hundreds of graves in the cemetery. Many graves had tombstones erected over them.

The names of the deceased were written on marble stones upon some of the tombs. The dates on which they were born and died were also clearly inscribed. Yet some others had the words 'Family Tomb' written over them. All in all, I found an assortment of tombs there.

As I stood surveying those tombs, among thousands resting in their graves, the visage of two deceased persons popped up distinctly into my mind. They were not the wealthy, educated, or high pedigree persons of that area, but just ordinary.

One of them was Kochunni Upadesi. He was a six-foot-tall, stocky man with a flowing beard. His memory filled my heart with peace. He died of a snake-bite.

Once he was a cancer patient, but miraculously healed. And thus his life turned about towards the path of God. He shone brightly as a light of the land.

I doubt there was another person who loved and trusted others like him. He was of a sterling character. Although thousands lay in the cemetery, the face of this man and memories about him came rushing into my mind. And that is because he was a beacon of goodness.

Every day, hundreds of thousands are born and die in this world. They include billionaires, political leaders, and the rich. But we forget all of them soon after they are dead and gone. The society and individuals forget even their bereaved families. But we can never forget some people and their faces, howsoever poor they might have been. However much we try, we can never forget them. And that is because their character was so exemplary.

What do the people around you say about you? Will they say that you are a person who can be trusted? Or instead, will they say something like 'Oh, you mean that guy? If you move closely with him, you will land in a soup. He can't be trusted. He is a cheater, double-faced . . .' People will rate you based on their own experiences with you.

I know a man who holds a very responsible position in a charity organization. One day a man approached him to solve a problem related to the parish.

This responsible person said: 'Aha! Is that so? Please don't do anything foolish. You don't have to do as they say. You have been appointed there by the Church as in-charge to discharge your full responsibilities. The responsibilities of your Church are vested in you. You don't have to be subordinate to anyone. Things must be done there in accordance with your decisions. Be bold.' The man was happy on hearing this.

That same evening, four people from the opposite group came to meet this same leader to talk about the same problem the other group talked to him about.

He told them: 'Aha! How did that happen? Never give an inch. The plot and buildings belong to the Church. You are all responsible for that. So, the committee members can't do as they like without consulting you. Those who come to preach or sing there must do just that and go. They have no right there beyond that. You are responsible for everything else. You are responsible to keep an account of everything including a small nail.' The party went happily, telling each other that the leader's thoughts matched theirs.

Weeks passed by. Once in a while, each party would come to meet him. He would always support the visiting party and talk against the opposite party. Eventually the problem became serious, and the leader came to solve it.

Both parties appeared and started to narrate their issues. As the consultations progressed, the secret got uncovered.

The party that had first approached the leader spoke thus: 'Didn't he tell us to do this?' The opposite party replied: 'He told us the very same thing!' Finally, these two parties that were sworn enemies, like a snake and a mongoose, became united and drove the leader out from their midst.

What actually happened here? A man who acts as an opportunist just to please people and earn their accolades, he criticizes others. No one knows about it for the time being. But in the long run, everyone comes to know about it—that he is a double-faced deceiver who is faithful to no one.

Are we truly faithful to the people around us, at our workplace and our friends? Can they trust us in any situation, even in the darkest night?

There lived a king in 971–993 BC. He was possibly the richest king and wisest. One day two mothers came to him both pleading for this king to resolve a conflict between them. His name was King Solomon.

It so happened that they both had given birth to babies. While they were sleeping, one of the children died. The mother that saw her child is dead, decided to exchange her lifeless baby with the other child. In the morning, these women got into a serious emotional matter with each other. Each one claiming the living child was hers and no one could resolve the problem. These two women and the dead body and the living child were brought before the king to hear the case. After hearing the two mothers' emotionally moving story, the wise king gave the order to cut the living child into half and give each mother one part of the severed child. Suddenly the real mother of the child cried out, 'please, your majesty, let her have the child, I don't want my child to be killed . . .' Strange, the fake mother was happy with the king's decision. You guessed it right, the wise king Solomon responded saying, 'Don't kill the child, give the child to the lady who pleaded not to cut the child into halves. She is the real true mother.'[1]

The lesson for all of us is to grow in wisdom and understanding so that we can be loving and kind to all based on truth and mercy. God is the source of all that is good and right and we must depend on Him for wisdom, beyond our own human limitations.

Educating the mind is knowledge, but educating the heart is wisdom and the classroom you learn that is humility.

29

Mend Your Mind to Make Your Life

As a youth, I worked in Delhi for some time, doing social welfare activities. An incident that happened inside a public transport bus still stays fresh in my mind as though it took place yesterday.

Two seats ahead of my seat, a young man and his wife were travelling. After a while, this woman looked back sharply twice at another young man occupying the next rear row. Seeing her stare in this manner, it occurred to me that something was wrong. As the bus negotiated two more sharp curves, I saw the woman whispering something in her husband's ear.

The enraged husband turned back, caught the young man in the rear by his collar, and asked: 'Hey, can't you behave properly? Why do you keep pulling women's hair when you are travelling?'

Taken aback at this sudden assault, this young man was dismayed and began sweating profusely. There was a mother sitting beside this young man and witnessing these developments. She instantly touched the hair of the woman in front and said to her: 'Daughter, look here. Your hair got entangled on a nail at the back of this seat and got tugged. This young boy is innocent.'

When I looked again, I found tears falling from that young man's eyes.

We too are like this sometimes. We react without knowing the facts. And that ends in tears for some others.

Wrong thinking and thoughtless response are equally harmful. We humans are constantly thinking. That is what distinguishes us from other species. But we must take care to ensure that our thoughts are always such that they lead us towards goodness and progress, and not towards evil and destruction.

Blaise Pascal, a seventeenth-century French mathematician and philosopher, once said: 'Man is only a reed, the weakest in nature, but he is a thinking reed.'[1]

God created us out of dust, and not of gold or silver. Our life may be a broken reed. It may be like a weak reed that snaps and falls when a strong wind blows. Nonetheless, as this thinker said, we are reeds that God created for the purpose of thinking.

A reed is of no value by itself. However, we have been created in the likeness of God, and our dignity consists in our thinking.

Another secret behind a happy life is that we must think as we should.

Once a wit asked Sir Isaac Newton, 'Sir, how did you discover the Theory of Gravity?'

'Gravity? Yes, I thought a lot about it,' replied Newton.

James Allen said, 'As a man thinketh in his heart, so shall he be.'[2]

Ralph Waldo Emerson said thus: 'A man is what he thinks about all day long.'[3]

The Buddha said, 'We are shaped by our thoughts; we become what we think. When the mind is pure, joy follows like a shadow that never leaves.'[4]

The entire humanity moves towards progress or destruction according to their thoughts. Even war and peace are basically founded on man's thoughts. Your family life will either be joyful or without peace according to your thinking. Our dealings with family members vary in accordance with our thoughts.

A loving word is a seed of love. Wherever it falls, it sprouts forth love and joy. Likewise, anger, animosity, and hatred also produce quick fruits. Wherever it falls, tranquillity is lost.

Whenever you see a person, if you repeatedly ask him a hundred times, 'Hey! What's the matter with you? Are you unwell? Your face looks pulled down!' then that healthy person will suddenly fall ill. If we say to ourselves 'Oh, I'm tired' and curl up in a bed, we are bound to become a patient sooner than later. Our thoughts affect our body as well.

When our mind is filled with a sense of fear and failure, words that flow from our mouth will be in tune with it. It influences our actions. We become suspicious about everyone and cannot trust anyone; we lose our calmness; we become touchy and easily provoked, and we wish to live alone as in an island.

Most often, we fail not because of others or due to adverse circumstances. But rather, it is due to our response to such events or problems. To put it more lucidly, the cause of your unhappiness is the way those external circumstances reflect upon your sphere of thinking.

We must learn to calmly think and act instead of suddenly blowing out like a volcano. We must resolve to become a part of the solution rather than a part of the problem.

Good, creative thinking don't come without effort. The Holy Scripture tells us, as command, to think on positive things not negative thoughts of failure and doom.

'Whatever is true,

whatever is noble,

whatever is right,

whatever is pure,

whatever is lovely,

whatever is admirable—if anything is excellent or
    praiseworthy—

think about such things.'[5]

Application:

Avoid negative friends, gossipmongers etc.—they are carriers of vipers that kills.

See the good in others and praise them for it.

Read books that uplift and give motivation to build hope in us.

Try to see the positive side of every adverse thing you face in life.

30

A True Friend

There are many significant sayings about the futility of greed and wealth.

'He who is not contented with what he has, would not be contented with what he would like to have,'—Socrates[1]

'Never trade your soul for money because you would never be able to trade that money to get your soul back. Money is good, but it's definitely not everything.' —Edmond Mbiaka[2]

Such proverbs highlight the emptiness and meaninglessness of riches!

Once, a billionaire was stricken by cancer. His people took him to a medical college hospital. He had only one son, a doctor. His daughter-in-law too was a doctor. His son and wife worked in a well-known hospital at a distant place.

This billionaire had lost his wife some years back and he was staying alone in his mansion.

He lay at the medical college hospital, awaiting death. He had so much wealth that his grave could be covered in gold. But neither his son and daughter-in-law nor his kith and kin could save him. There was a poor man who stayed by his side and constantly looked after him day and night.

There is a story behind this poor man's willingness to care for him. He was a tenant in the billionaire's land. Many years back, this rich man called the police and got the poor tenant forcibly evicted from his land, and then set his thatched hut on fire.

When the tenant was young, he used to take care of the billionaire's affairs and in return the rich man would help him in difficult times. He had not forgotten these things, and that little flame of love still remained alive in his heart.

So, he did not engage in any quarrel or legal case with the billionaire. He remained loyal to his previous landlord and never uttered a word against him. Now being homeless the poor man built a small hut in the Government surplus land and began to live there.

The rich man had all the comforts and luxuries of life that he could ever want. He had massive wealth—all for his only son. The sad thing was, even when his father was sick and dying in the hospital, he would not even once visit his father in the hospital.

Question: What is more valuable here—love or wealth? The answer is obvious.

This bed-ridden rich man lost his ability to speak. With tears in his eyes, he would simply look at the poor attendant's face. His eyes seemed to silently speak these words to him: 'Please forgive me. I did you wrong. Money, power, property, and palatial buildings are all worthless. Love alone is valuable. And I now know it, but it is too late.'

Money and comforts are necessary for our lives. We need food to eat, clothes to wear, and a house to live in, and a vehicle to travel. But above all these, we must attach importance to kindness and love.

Assume that you are working in a company or establishment. If you have loyalty towards them, you will never take pleasure in their problems and sorrows, difficulties and downfall.

Let me share the story of a man who was good, sincere, and hardworking. He went to Mumbai in search of a job. But he could not find one.

A man who knew him started an establishment. He said: 'I have great faith in you. I am investing this money only for your sake.' This man became a Manager in that firm. The company grew and started earning good revenue.

Before long, another company invited this man to work for them. They offered him up to five times the salary he was currently earning.

But he replied: 'I thank you for the offer. I like your company, and have high regards for you. You are all good people. But I cannot leave my boss who trusted me and invested his money for my sake. Although this firm is rather small, my boss is one who has sacrificed much, having put his faith in me. Even if my benefits may be small, I will not forsake the man who trusted me, and go away. Sorry, I can't join you. Thank you for your offer, but sorry, I can't accept it.'

What a gem of a character this man was! What about you? Can people vouch for you that you will not abandon ship when it is in jeopardy?

I happened to read a true story about a man published in a local newspaper. He was picked up by the police in connection with some case and taken away. He had to spend a few days in jail.

But the interesting part of this news story was about his dog. The dog loved its master very much. And the man loved it as much.

When the policemen arrested this man and was taken to the police station, this dog followed them. They had to cross a river. They got into a boat, but did not let the dog get into it. So, the dog swam across the river and kept following them.

On seeing this, some people tried to dissuade the dog from trailing them. They threw stones at it, but it evaded them by running away. It kept following them again. The man was remanded and had to spend eight days in jail.

Finally, the dog reached the police station. For as many as eight days, it sat in front of the jail without moving anywhere. When its master was released from jail, the dog joined him and proceeded to their house. How great was this dog's love for its master!

This dog could have rationalized, thinking, 'Oh! What can I do? My master is gone. Probably he got into some mess. Let him put up with it.' But, as it loved its master, the dog did not leave him even though it had to swim across the river, and suffer other hardships. It stayed with him and would not desert him.

Here is the gist of a letter I received: This man had three daughters. All of them were grown up and well above the marriageable age. One fine morning, he vanished, leaving his wife and daughters alone in the thatched hut.

Several years have passed, but there has been no trace of him or his whereabouts. Obviously, he was facing a host of predicaments: He had to get his three daughters married, and maintain his family; but he had no wherewithal to do all that. Nevertheless, we can only imagine the burdens, difficulties, sufferings and agony his heart-broken family would have gone through. And how excruciating the distress of the mother who had given birth to them! No doubt, he had his own problems. But, instead of sharing in their pains and trying to make his own family secure, he simply deserted them.

Such incidents are not uncommon.

Here is another story of a household. The husband lost one leg and an eye in an accident. His wife's love has now turned cold. He once had a top class job and tons of money. But the company went broke. Everything crashed to the ground. And now his wife and children do not want him.

True love and loyalty means, we don't desert the ones we love during times of their sufferings and setbacks.

For thousands of years, an unwritten rule has been voluntarily passed on by captains who were steering ships all their life across great oceans and seas. If a ship runs into rough weather and is about to sink, the captain would instruct all on board to first escape. He would lower small life-boats into the water and ensure that everyone got into them safely. Only after ensuring that not a single life was left in the sinking ship would the captain look for a way to save his own life. Never would he attempt to first get himself into a life-boat and escape, leaving everyone else in the sinking ship to die.

A true friend is one who stands by us in peril.

31

What You Can't Buy with Money

Now that you have suffered some losses and setbacks, being instigated by some people, you are talking against your benefactors. You keep criticizing them, and have become their enemy privately and publicly.

Let me share the experiences of a person known to me. He had been working for a company for many long years. They paid him a fairly good salary. He lived with his wife and two school-going children. They had a car of their own. All in all, they were among good days.

Whenever we met, he used to happily talk about the virtues of his boss and the strengths of his company. After about four months, when I happened to run to him, his face was fallen and lacklustre, as though bitten by an owl. I asked him, 'What's the matter?'

'Oh! The less said the better! Things don't look good.'

'What happened?' I asked with concern.

'Oh, I'm quitting my job and going to the Gulf. Not that I am keen to go, but I have no choice.'

I asked: 'When you have a job and livelihood opportunities here, why should you throw them up and go away?'

He instantly replied: 'I'm happy here. I have a job with good salary. And my wife need not work. But they were unjust to me.'

'Unjust?'

'Yeah, they gave promotion to my juniors and ignored me. I can't work here any longer,' he said with some chagrin.

'Did they reduce your salary or allowances?'

'No.'

'Then why should you quit?'

'It's degrading to work here anymore.'

I tried to pep him up with some soothing counsel and advice, but in vain. Finally, he quit the job.

Think about it.

He had been working there for long years and earned good positions and ranks. He was well-educated. But he did not like the fact that some of his colleagues got a promotion. He took it as an insult. His grouse was that he was ignored for the promotion. So, he went around criticizing his company and its managers. He decided that he would not work there any longer.

Circumstances may arise when you have no choice but to quit your job. But, if your heart sinks when others earn a better compensation or position, it does not reflect loyalty on your part.

There is a world-renowned Hospital and Medical College in India that was started by Christian Missionary that came to serve the poor and needy in our land. Missionary doctors and nurses from America and various other countries worked hard to build this hospital. Many people from Kerala also work there.

One day, as we were walking along that way, we found a huge commotion going on in front of the hospital. A man stood upon a table and, throwing his hand up into the air, kept shouting: 'Inquilab Zindabad' (long live the Revolution)! Hundreds of workers milling around him kept repeating the slogan in chorus. A black flag was planted nearby. This man had mobilized these workers to agitate against the establishment.

This has been happening at many other locations for many factories like major paper mills etc. Ultimately, everything is shut down and things begin to rust and gather dust, and then become good for nothing. It may happen that, in certain situations, at your workplace, you do not always get what you deserve. What would be your response in this context?

Think of these disloyal people, when they first went for the job interview! Didn't they step into that job with a lot of apprehension and fear, saying things like 'Sir, please . . . I will do the best for your company. I will do whatever you say.' What happened as time moved on? They have forgotten the help they received. Agreed, that they were not getting a huge salary of lakhs. But at least they had a decent job and salary.

Now that this individual did suffer some losses and setbacks, being instigated by others he began talking against his benefactors. He keeps criticizing them, and has become their enemy privately and publicly.

Consider loyalty and faithfulness as most important and valuable. At times we may lose our rights and benefits. The question is, time like that, will we remain loyal and maintain our integrity?

This is a true story from ancient history. There lived a man named Joseph. He had parents and siblings. They lived happily; there were no issues. But as time passed, their mother died. His brothers began to detest him. Gradually their jealousy and hatred grew. And they sold him as a slave in Egypt.

He worked as a slave in the house of an official of King Pharaoh. But Joseph honoured God. This young man who had done no wrong worked as a slave and struggled. There was no end to his misery. Based on his wife's complaint, his master misunderstood Joseph. He was accused of a crime he did not commit and shut up in a prison cell—not for a year or two, but for thirteen long years. Rejected by all, Joseph lay in this cell, and his hair and beard grew long.

But in God's good time, Joseph was set free. Eventually, through a series of miracles he became the Prime Minister of the ancient Egypt.

Even today, there are many innocent people languishing in jails for crimes that they never committed. This is the reality not merely in our country, but across different parts of the world.

There must have been many other prisoners in prison with Joseph. They included murderers, burglars, thieves, traitors, and those guilty of treason. But never once during those thirteen long years did Joseph utter a word accusing his master or mistress who had betrayed him.

When Joseph came out of the prison after his jail term, the woman and her husband who had falsely foisted charges on him and sent him to prison were very much present there along with their family. He could have done anything to them in vengeance, or even destroyed them. He could have said to himself, 'They put me in prison for thirteen years. Let me now have them put in prison for a few dozen years.' Not once did Joseph talk against them or criticize them, or contemplate taking revenge upon them.

As we traverse through the story, we come across many others who had persecuted Joseph. His own brothers who had once set a trap to destroy him and even take his life, years go by finally a time comes, driven by starvation his brothers came to Egypt to buy food and stood before Joseph, the Prime Minister with folded hands. But they did not know that it was the very same Joseph, their own brother that they did wrong to and sold him as a slave to Egypt.

Humanly speaking, it was a golden opportunity to teach them a lesson, but Joseph did not once think of harming them. What a great heart he had!

When a man is denied his rights, is misunderstood, and when people work against him, he suffers everything without a thought of wreaking vengeance—a man with such a character is called 'faithful' before God's eyes. Joseph's life illustrates this best.

There was once a man who was very fond of dogs. He used to buy the best of breeds by paying a substantial price. He would feed them with meat, fish, and milk, and he built separate kennels for each of them.

Among them, he particularly likes one dog called Jack. He kept growing quickly, eating meat, fish, and all.

He loved his master very much and accompanied him wherever he went. If he sensed any impending danger to his master at any time, Jack would be ready to even sacrifice his life for the master's sake.

As time moved on, this man bought another dog of a new breed—the best breed in the country in those days. Only a few of these new breed dogs were available then, as they were top rated. He paid a large sum of money to get this puppy. After all, having bought it at such a high price, he brought it up with matching types of food and nourishment.

Now, Jack slept on the cement floor. But the new dog, a foreign breed, slept on a costly carpet and ate special food, meat, milk and other stuff. And it rapidly grew big in a matter of time.

However, there was no change in Jack's behaviour. He was still faithful. He watched over his master's house and premises, and discharged his duties meticulously.

There was a minor difference in the behaviour of these two dogs. As for Jack, he loved his master deeply, and besides, his dedication did not diminish a wee bit.

But the other dog was of a little higher class. He was not as dedicated as Jack, and moreover, he did not like to go around with his master. He was more interested in listening to others as they commented about his gait, food habits, comfortable life, and so on.

One day, the master went out on a casual stroll. As usual, Jack followed, softly walking behind him. The master was not aware of this. Suddenly, someone shouted: 'Run, run. Here comes a mad dog.'

A timely alert! Yes, a rabid dog was indeed heading in their direction. It was fast approaching, with its tail hanging, tongue jutting out, and slimy froth flowing from its mouth. As soon as Jack sighted it, he lunged forward ahead of his master and started running.

Jack shot forth like lightning and grabbed the rabid dog with his mouth and felled it to the ground within moments. People gathered around. They were amazed and said: 'Oh! How many people got bitten by this mad dog! Now we can relax.'

A little later, they became rather serious and their conversation took on a different tone. Some of them said that the master must kill Jack as he was bitten by the rabid dog. He thought for a while and said, 'Never. I won't kill Jack. I will save him by getting him anti-rabies shots.'

He continued: 'I have been breeding many dogs. Recently I bought a special breed for a hefty price. I am giving it the best of things as it wants. But I've never seen a dog that loves me as much as Jack. Never have I bred a dog that was ready to give its life for my sake.'

If Jack were to think like a man, he might have said, 'I have lived here all these days faithfully watching over my master. But still, I get only a cement floor to sleep on. Look at that chap. He is a big shot. He has a special house with a carpet, eats special eggs, milk, meat and all that. I don't even get enough food to eat. Let the mad dog bite him. I couldn't care less! I won't budge.' Jack could have simply stayed back, rationalising in this manner.

But this is not the mark of one who is loyal. His thoughts would be along these lines: 'Let others do as they please. Let them earn as much as they can. But I will always work faithfully wherever I am placed. I won't worry if I get less compensation or a lower position. Regardless of all that, I will remain faithful.' A person who works in this manner is the truly faithful and trustworthy one.

Whatever our work, and wherever we are placed, we must work sincerely without looking at the compensation we receive.

Once I read about R.V. Peter who is better known as the 'Postman's Brother.' He started to work as a postman in Kodaikanal in the year 1913. After serving in the Postal Department for sixty-eight years, he retired in 1981.

Peter won the Department's award seventeen times. In 1949, he earned the citation and a golden watch as gift from the Government of India for his distinguished service.[1]

He always kept his one-room post office neat and tidy. And he dealt with everyone lovingly. Peter was faithful in all things. And that is why everyone around him, and the world as such, honours him.

'There are people who may be earning salaries in five or six digits, who hold high positions, ranks and dignity. That doesn't worry me. I will do the work entrusted to me faithfully without looking at the reward,' such was his resolve.

When he retired, he had a meagre salary of Rs 210 per month. But the dignity and recognition he earned could never have been bought for money.

The world is starving for a few good men and women. Will you choose to be one?

32

Where the Freedom of Mind Begins

In December 1972, an incident occurred that hurt me deeply. A person, who had grossly misunderstood me and so harshly dealt with me as to cause me hurt and pain, finally wrote me a lengthy letter. As soon as I saw that voluminous letter containing many pages, my blood began to boil.

My mind was filled with rage and my heart was heavy with hatred. I was innocent and had no part whatsoever in the matter, but he misunderstood me and was treating me as though I was the culprit.

I filed that letter. Time moved on, and two years went by. The man who had misunderstood me finally realized that I was innocent. He mentioned it to a third party and hinted that his misunderstanding about me was a mistake.

I still remember how I pulled out his old letter from my file. It is hard to believe, but the moment I read through that letter again, the same pain, bitterness, resentment, rancour, and heaviness welled up within me just as it did when I had read it first. Immediately, I realized that it would not be prudent to harbour such thoughts.

So, I took that letter and tore it into pieces. I had kept on record the problems he created through what he had spoken about me and done to me. But one fine day I put an end to it. Because, love does not keep a count of faults.

It may be that you are still preserving in your hands and in the racks of your mind books of accusation running into hundreds of pages. Forgive and forget all the faults and transgressions of others, and never keep them on record. And then you will enjoy peace and health of mind and body.

Our state of mind is a vital component of a healthy life. Every matter that causes pain in our mind will invariably affect our thinking, our future, and our health. In order to keep our mental state pure, we ought to eliminate the bitterness and hatred that we have towards others. We must bid goodbye to rankling memories. Memories of old concerning our bitter experiences are indeed poison trees that will strangle us to death.

Once, a girl came to meet me. She was lean and lank, with a dark complexion and deep-set eyes. Her hair was swept back, but kept gambolling about. She wore a cheap beaded necklace, and had neither bangles nor a watch on her arms.

As soon as she entered, she said with tears in her eyes: 'Sir, I don't want to live any longer. I don't find any meaning in life.' I perceived a resolute ring in her voice.

Another girl who had come along with her sat in a chair a little away. I understood that the girl was seized by an obsession to end her life.

I asked her gently, 'Dear child, what's your problem? Why do you have such thoughts?'

Perhaps prompted by my gentle approach, she replied in a low voice: 'I've been suffering all these insults and mocking ever since I was born . . . And now they are looking to get me married. Most of the proposals don't click.'

'Why?' I probed.

She said: 'Sir, I was born on Chitthira (birth star). I grew up hearing that those born under this star would become a curse for the family.' I had heard of such local beliefs. She continued sharing her grief:

'My mother once said it would have been better if this damned girl had never been born. She said that a problem had cropped up in the family because of me. And thereafter, I had occasion to hear such comments once too often.'

She wiped her face and continued: 'All my marriage proposals are getting aborted because of my faulty birth star. I have realized one thing—that persons like me have no future. Sir, don't you agree that it's better for me to die?'

Here was a girl who was carrying the burden of an accursed birth star and determined to put an end to her life. I knew that her mother's old words of rebuke remained fresh in her mind and tormented her.

'If the circumstances of your life change for the better, won't you like to live?' I comforted her.

But she responded, 'This is my fate!'

'Would God have sent you into this world if He wanted you to die?'

She did not reply.

I said to her: 'This earth has enough room for all the people born under several stars.' She looked intently at me as I continued, 'Some people may consider us as born under accursed stars. But still, we are all God's children. He does not want us to be destroyed. Circumstances will change for the better. And you will lead a happy life.'

'I have no idea how that can ever happen,' she said nonchalantly.

I replied instantaneously, 'Chitthira star is actually not your problem.'

She looked eagerly at me and seemed keen to ask me something, but refrained.

I said, 'Your problem lies in your mother's words. Those words keep hurting you as haunting memories.'

Immediately, she buried her face in her palms and burst into tears. I let her cry as I was certain that her tears would bring her some solace. After a while, she wiped her face with her hands, looked at me, and said:

'I hate my mother most. She always keeps quarrelling with me about my birth star.'

Tell me, I asked her, 'Was it your fault that you were born under the Chitthira star?'

Her face lit up a wee bit. Trying to smile, she replied, 'No.'

'Should you suffer punishment for a fault that is not yours?'

She looked at me and shook her head.

'Suicide, blaming others, or living in solitude are not a solution. Instead, you must get rid of the negative thoughts that keep haunting you. Dream about a bright future, always think about the goodness in life. Look at the opportunities that life offers you.' She kept listening to me, and it seemed to give a new direction to her thoughts, howsoever little.

We continued our conversation for some more time. I gave her a book I authored, 'Love Yourself', and asked her to read it. I bid her goodbye with instructions that she must return after a week.

She came back after a week. Along with her were her mother and the girl who had accompanied her during the first visit. I got all the three seated together and talked with them. The mother realized the adverse consequences of the words of rebuke she had uttered. And the girl was able to forgive her mother. They left, dreaming of a bright future and good life ahead.

We must burn or destroy some letters that we preserve. And we must reject some memories that we nurse. We should never entertain a single thought that torments our mind. That is where the freedom of mind begins.

All that happens to us, even the worst experience happened for a reason, they are meant to teach us something and make our soul better.

33

The Incarnations of Mercy

Once a grown-up dog was watching a little puppy play. The puppy was circling around, trying to bite the edge of its own tail.

Big Dog asked: 'Hey, little one, What are you up to?'

Puppy: 'Big Brother, in the past few months, I've been thinking about the secret of real happiness.'

Big Dog: 'And did you find the result of your enquiry?'

Puppy: 'Sure. That's exactly what I'm trying to demonstrate. We dogs have the secret of happiness in our tails. And so, I'm trying to get hold of my tail somehow or other.'

Big Dog: 'Hey, do you know I used to think like you years ago? I kept going round and round—just to grab this happiness once. But finally, I realized that it was all futile. So, now I keep walking straight ahead, and my tail follows in tow.'

Big Dog continued: 'Mut, there's no need for you to circle around like this and waste your time. If your tail holds the secret to your happiness, you only have to walk straight and your tail will simply follow you.'

Doesn't it sound right? For a little peace, people are going round and round, and running helter-skelter.

If you ask a drunkard as to why he keeps drinking regularly, his reply would be on these lines, 'Oh, what shall I say? I drink a peg or two for a little solace. I down a draught just to forget my problems for a while, and to get over my smarting memories.'

A few other alcoholics would respond with these words: 'If I gulp down a pint of this elixir, I can have a hearty laugh, and sing a song at the top of my voice . . .'

Why do people smoke cannabis? An inexplicable pleasure, a high feeling, some joy . . . We all live in a world filled with pain and suffering; so everyone looks for a way to gain a bit of peace and joy.

I heard of an incident recently. An affluent man joined with a few of his friends and soon spent all his wealth, drinking like a fish. Now he is on death-bed, afflicted with liver cirrhosis. He can hardly recognize people. According to his doctors, he has only a few days left to live on this earth.

Why did that man start drinking? Obviously, for a little peace, and a bit of happiness.

A person who experiences real happiness does not complain under any situation. His life is controlled by God. 'My life is in the hands of God. My God will not let anything evil happen to me.'

A person who lives gratefully with this knowledge is the one who experiences true joy. Such a person will never wander about in search of happiness.

Do we get happiness by chasing after money? If a man is covered with ten thousand bundles of Rs 500 currency notes, he would still groan from under the load, saying that he did not have enough! That is the plight of man.

Someone has done you a favour. But, are you able to say a word of thanks to the benefactor? Somebody has taught you something that you did not know. Will you tell him, 'Sir, thanks a lot'? Your parents have done for you everything you needed. Are you able to tell them, 'I am grateful to you, Mom and Dad, for all that you have done'? Another person gave you something. Did you say, 'Brother, I am so grateful'?

Humility and joy are the signs of a life of gratitude. But one can only fail if one frantically wanders about in search of happiness in life. Let me illustrate through a story.

Many years ago, a man gifted his son with a precious watch. It was a golden pocket watch. He called his son and told him: 'Son, look. My grandfather gave this watch to my father. My dad gave it to me. And now I'm giving it to you. Take good care of it, son.'

He said, 'Okay, Dad' and kept it safely in his room.

After two weeks, his son put the watch into his pocket and showed it to his friends. As they were playing beside a saw-mill with its front yard filled with dry leaves, saw dust, and trash, somehow he lost the watch as it fell out from his pocket. Along with his friends he searched for it all around the place, but could not find it. He was greatly troubled and on the verge of tears.

Finally, all his friends left and went their ways. Then he thought to himself, 'My friends are all gone. I am going to stand here quietly. Then I will be able to hear the tick-tock sound of the watch.' So he stood still and tuned his ears to hear the ticking sound. In this way, he was able to retrieve his lost watch.

Imagine the immense joy and excitement of this boy at that moment. He jumped up in joy and went home happily.

In the same manner, we all wish to have happiness in our life. Why do people go to foreign lands and earn hundreds of thousands of rupees working there? They do it for the sake of building a magnificent house, to wear expensive apparels, and to own properties that they see around and to find happiness through all that.

But, what is reality? In this mad rush and rat-race, you have lost your peace of mind somewhere along the way. And you are searching along all the ways that you have traversed. Finally, you are crying and fretting like the boy who lost his watch.

How can we regain the joy that we have lost? Simply stand still and listen quietly for a while as the boy did. Remember the blessings that God has showered upon you. And then the tick-tock sound will begin to fall upon your ears. We must go beyond our problems and pains, and acknowledge God's blessings.

We must nurture a heart that is filled with gratitude. And then we will regain the happiness that we once lost.

'Gratitude is a powerful catalyst for happiness. It's the spark that lights a fire of joy in your soul.'[1]

We have around us numerous people who are seeking happiness and comfort. We must be able to transfer the blessings and graces that God has bestowed upon us to them as well. And that is where we shall find true joy.

Once I was in conversation with someone about leprosy patients in India.

He said, 'My people join me to spend our time loving, helping, and sharing God's love with those lepers.'

He has appointed trained personnel to nurse, teach, love, and comfort lepers in over forty colonies.

During our conversation, he opened his bag and showed me some photographs he had kept therein. One photo showed some leprosy patients. Some of them had many of their fingers mutilated; one had three-quarters of his nose chopped; a few had their ears missing, and yet some others had large bandages here and there on their body.

He stood in their midst, with his hands upon their shoulders, as though he was one among them. He did not stand a foot away from them, considering that they were lepers after all. His eyes did not display the slightest trace of repulsion that one normally feels towards lepers. Instead, I could only see the glow of love and the light of compassion upon his face.

I remembered St Teresa of Calcutta (Mother Teresa) who gave loving care to lepers and the destitute people in the streets of Calcutta.

The committed lives of people like Mother Teresa influenced me so much that I was able to serve lepers in several colonies of leprosy patients in Purulia in West Bengal and other states. Mother Teresa is no more. But their works of charity have not come to an end. Mother Teresa's mission has not ceased either. I know that the incarnations of mercy have no death.

Be kind.

34

When the Doctor Falls Sick

Rajan was a reputed doctor. One of my friends phoned and informed me that Dr Rajan was in critical condition at the medical college hospital. I asked him what this doctor was ailing from. He answered that it was liver cirrhosis arising from consuming illicit alcohol and drugs.

I decided to visit him. I located the hospital room where he was lying and reached his bedside. Years ago when I had first met Dr Rajan, he was handsome and healthy.

My mind was rattled as I saw this doctor lying so emancipated and lifeless. I found it hard to understand as to how a doctor who knew very well about the harmful effects of drugs ended up in such a pathetic condition.

With sunken eyes, cheeks stuck to the bones, and overgrown hair and beard, his frame looked grotesque. I could not but let out a sigh as I saw his wife standing by.

Once a healthy woman, she also appeared to be in a pitiable shape now. And as I looked upon their exhausted and pale children, I gauged the depths of their misery.

When he could work no longer, it triggered a financial collapse. When he realized that he had lost his health and become financially broke, he wished to come out of the clutches of drugs and alcoholism. In his own strength, he could not come out of it.

I approached his bedside and called him by name. He opened his eyes and looked into my face. When I told him that I was there to see him and to pray for him, he burst into tears and said: 'Oh! I have ruined the life of my wife and children. Due to my bad habits, they have been reduced to poverty, with no one to depend on. I have wasted my life and lifespan. I know there's no deliverance for me. But, will God ever forgive me?'

Being a medical doctor, he should have been living happily with dignity and prosperity; but now he lay there helpless like a shredded old piece of rag! I felt very sad on hearing this news. How I wish this educated man had lived a bit more wisely!

Somehow in my heart I felt the prayers of his dear wife and children are heard by Almighty and bring healing and hope for this family. I took long time to talk to him of spiritual realities and how God can heal him and give him a new beginning.

I told him the story of a man who was sick and dying for thirty-eight years with no hope of recovery and how Jesus healing him as recorded in the Holy Scriptures. He listened with such hope and began to focus his thinking on God's love and mercy, not on his sin and failure. Believe it or not, in a mysterious way I felt God was in that room and I was there to represent God's love visibly for this man. I laid my hand on his forehead and prayed for God to heal him. I ended my prayer as the Holy Scripture says, asked God for his healing in Jesus' name. As we Orthodox Christians do, I traced the sign of the Cross three times on his forehead as a sign of his healing and recovery.

Soon, things began to change. In a month's time, Dr Rajan was slowly getting his strength back. Finally, he was fully healed.

All you can say, God loves all people and when we call on Him, He will help us.

Today, not only he is a healthy man, but his family is doing well by God's grace.

This is a lesson for all of us. Never give up hope. God is on our side and we should turn to Him not only in our bad times but always in all our ways.

Some years back, a man came to see me wanting to make his confession. It seemed that he wanted to tell me something, but his feet were wobbling, and his speech was slurred. As he came closer to me, I realized he was under the influence of drugs or alcohol.

Somehow he blurted out: 'Father, I've been waiting here for some time to see you. I'm a drunkard. Please forgive me. I'm the headmaster of a High School. I used to listen to your Spiritual Journey radio programme daily.

'But I'm a cursed man. I have no peace of mind. I have a lot of things to talk with Father . . . What must I do to be delivered from this bondage? I want to live. Please help me . . .'

Then he started to cry. He was in such a condition that there was little I could do. The next forty-five minutes or so he poured out his broken heart and all the terrible sins he had committed. I listened with empathy and silently prayed all through for God to have mercy on him.

In the end, when he finished, I asked him to repeat a simple prayer after me, for him to ask God for forgiveness. He did. I professed forgiveness of God and blessed him for a new beginning. Thank God, he was totally transformed by God's mercy and found a new beginning and hope.

Please remember, God your Creator is not against you. He loves you and when in need of anything, any problem you face, talk to God as you would talk to a friend. He will answer. When all is said and done, God is our only hope.

The White Elephant

I heard about a medical doctor who worked day and night, with one aim: to make as much money he can in a short time. He makes visits to three-four hospitals daily, driving hundreds of kilometres each day to meet his assignments. One day a young doctor asked him, 'Doctor, you look so wiped out and tensed-what happened?' The senior doctor responded saying, 'I am in such debt, I have to work to make ends meet.' To further question, 'why he needed so much money, since he was drawing very handsome salary' the response totally surprised the young doctor when this restless doctor said, 'I got a white elephant to take care of . . . I am under curse, what to do?'

Before I go further, I need to tell you what his 'white elephant' is all about.

In ancient Siam (now Thailand), white elephants were regarded as sacred animals. Usually kings and very rich people used to own these animals. To possess a white elephant was regarded (and is still regarded in Thailand and Burma) as a sign that the monarch reigned with justice and power and being blessed with peace and prosperity. In fact sometimes the kings named themselves after these elephants. These elephants were considered sacred and so they had people to take care of them, were never allowed to work and also had religious symbolism to them.

Once in a while, in order to show his great love and regard for someone, the king would gift one of these precious animals to a person. So if you had a white elephant it meant that you were greatly admired and honoured in that land. But there also used to be a curious custom. The king used to give two or three white elephants to someone who he didn't like! That sounds strange, right? Why would a king give such a highly valuable, prized procession to someone whom he thoroughly detested? The reason was that, if you owned this animal, you could not sell it. You also could not make it do any work. You had to take special care to feed it, have special people appointed to bathe it and make sure the white elephant was being taken care of well. Now this meant a huge amount of financial burden for the owner. Even a wealthy person would struggle to have enough financial resources to take care one white elephant, let alone two or three. So a 'white elephant' instead of bringing peace and happiness, in this case would bring about the financial ruin of this person this gift was meant to destroy! In other words, 'white elephant' is anything that people buy or build or own, which was supposed to bring happiness and peace, but ended up ruining the person owning it, as he or she cannot take care of it.[1]

Now back to the doctor and his 'white elephant.' Some time back he and his wife (who also was a doctor) decided to build a house. They made plans for their house and finally settled on an elaborate plan for a spacious house. When the budget was calculated, they didn't actually have enough money with them to build it. 'But no problem; I can take a bank loan,' he told himself and since both of them were successful doctors, surely they could easily pay off the loans. So the construction on their dream house started. The construction took longer than expected, and as time went by the cost of finishing also went higher and higher. Every time they thought about escalating costs, they reasoned that it's ok. Finally when they finished their house, they had to take much more loan than they had anticipated. This meant they had to pay much more money each month than calculated. In turn, that meant they had to make much more money than they were earlier making. So what do you do? Run around and make as much money as you possibly can!

This was what the doctor was doing now. Then he looked at me and said, 'Please don't make the mistake I made. I live in this house now but I have no peace, all I can think about is paying off the next loan. I don't have time for anything, no time for family, children, relaxation or shopping. I leave early from my home, drive so much, go to several hospitals and finally reach exhausted and late to my home, only to start the cycle again next day.' I then asked him, 'Doctor why did you have to build such a big house? Your house is much too big for your needs; with six rooms, 5,000 square feet, and a lawn big enough to play football, it was a monstrous house!' He looked at me and smiled. He said his wife was a 'showy' person. She always wanted to show others how wealthy and how big a house they had. So it was she who insisted to having such a big house and he had given in to the demand. So now, the house, which was meant to be a home, is a burden—ruining their lives and family.

This is not only with the case of buying or building a house. It extends to many possessions one owns, like vehicles, appliances, electronic gadgets etc. I'm sure all of us can say about at least one thing we bought – Oh, I wish I hadn't bought that. But why do we end up doing that? Why do we buy things we don't need? Why do we build things much bigger than our necessity and why do we ruin ourselves by owning white elephants?

We humans driven by our primate passions believe falsely that 'a man's life consists in the abundance of his or her possessions.' We feel that bigger is better and that more expensive means more valuable. We like to show others who we are, how important we are and try to get others to respect us by showing off what we own. For men, this may be watches, expensive pens, latest electronic gadgets or branded clothing; while for women it might be perfumes, jewellery, clothes they wear or even bags they flaunt! But in reality we are only trying to hide the vacuum or emptiness inside us with external things. It's a like a doctor prescribing an expensive pair of trousers for a patient who needs surgery to fix this broken leg! Think about it for a moment, do all these 'external' things give us peace and satisfaction and contentment? Maybe for a short while, but soon like a bubble it bursts, only to leave us emptier than before.

During the early years when I was doing the daily radio programs, I heard about a man who got married and went to Kuwait, leaving his wife behind. He would come to visit his wife one month a year. He did for the next forty years or so. Meanwhile they had two daughters born and grew up without their father . . . and went on to their studies, mostly staying at college hostels etc.

Finally the man resigned and came home. With the huge salary he made all these years, he was able to acquire much property and also build a house nothing less than a huge mansion. The sad thing is, after one month of his returning home after retirement, he had a cardiac arrest and died! When I heard that story, I said to myself, what for he spent his entire life to make money and . . . the material things that he could not take with him!

Greed kills our life. Life is more than the material things. No wonder, Jesus one time said, 'What shall it profit a man if he gain the whole world and loose his own soul?'

It is a beautiful life when we can live with contentment.

Another occasion, Christ, speaking of the dangers of greed, said a parable:

'Someone in the crowd said to him, 'Teacher, tell my brother to divide the inheritance with me.'

Jesus replied, 'Man, who appointed me a judge or an arbiter between you?' Then he said to them, 'Watch out! Be on your guard against all kinds of greed; life does not consist in an abundance of possessions.'

And he told them this parable: 'The ground of a certain rich man yielded an abundant harvest. He thought to himself, 'What shall I do? I have no place to store my crops.'

'Then he said, "This is what I'll do. I will tear down my barns and build bigger ones, and there I will store my surplus grain." And I'll say to myself, "You have plenty of grain laid up for many years. Take life easy; eat, drink and be merry."'

'But God said to him, "You fool! This very night your life will be demanded from you. Then who will get what you have prepared for yourself?"'

'This is how it will be with whoever stores up things for themselves but is not rich toward God.'[2]

Holy Scripture warns us: 'The love of money is the root of all evil.'[3]

A lesson to learn!

35

Compassion

I can't remember when or where I read the story, probably when I lived in Germany. It's a story about a rich man who lived in a German village.

This rich man had a desire in his heart—that he should do something charitable and helpful for others. Around this time, the statement of Christ caught his attention, 'When you give to the needy, do not let your left hand know what your right hand is doing, so that your alms may be in secret.'[1]

This wealthy man talked to a poor man in the neighbouring village and told him in confidence: 'Can you please do me a favour?'

He replied respectfully: 'Please let me know what I can do for you.'

The rich man said: 'We must help the poor people that live in my village and your village. We have hundreds of desperately poor families living all around us.'

'But Sir, I don't have any means to help these people. I'm myself a poor, starving man,' replied the poor man.

'Don't worry! I am rich and I have plenty to spare. But none should know that I am giving away this money,' explained the rich man. 'Every week, I will hand over some money to you. You must distribute it to the poor. But you must not disclose to anyone I am the one doing it.' The poor man agreed.

Months and years went by.

This impoverished man started to help hundreds of poor people every week. He would give them food, clothes, medicines, and so on after ascertaining their needs. News about this spread like wildfire throughout the land.

People spoke to each other in this manner: 'Look, this man is poor. But he is an angel. In the neighbouring village lives a filthy rich man in a mansion, wallowing in wealth and luxurious living. A greedy devil that don't care for us poor people! Wait till God sends him to hell.' They kept on denigrating and talking ill of the rich man.

On hearing such things, the poor man was greatly troubled. He wanted to reveal the truth to everyone. But he remembered that he had promised never to disclose this secret.

Time moved on. One day, suddenly the rich man died. A large number of people gathered to take part in the funeral rites. Among them were the wealthy, political leaders, and so on. This poor man was also there. As the deceased was a billionaire, the media also turned up in good numbers.

Obituary speeches were in progress one after the other. The poor man approached the parish priest and said: 'Father, please give me ten minutes. I want to share something about the deceased.'

The priest replied: 'Oh! What would you say about him?' 'Please, Father. Give me just five minutes,' pleaded the poor man.

At his insistence, the priest gave him a few minutes to speak. He stood before the throng gathered there and began to speak: 'Friends, all these years I have been helping many people by giving them money. I wiped the tears from many eyes. Many children are now going to school. Homeless people now have a house of their own. Sick people have received medicines, and today they are living in good health. Friends, but I didn't do all that. It was all done by the man who now lies here dead.'

He continued to narrate all that had happened. The listeners were astounded. There was a pin-drop silence. Finally, thousands of people flocked to his grave. After the funeral, they said: 'Actually, here rests an angel who loved us.'

After some years, this poor man also died. He was buried in a grave beside the rich man's tomb. Generations will never forget the tombs of these two great men.

After the rich man's death, the poor man would often lament: 'Alas! If only I were able to say all these things when he was alive!'

The people would then console him, saying: 'Don't burden yourself with such thoughts. You kept the word you gave to him. You spoke entirely what you had to speak at the right time. You acted to uphold the dignity and honour of that great generous soul.

This rich man truly understood the meaning of kindness.

While there are very kind and generous people, sad to say, there are horribly self-centered people that don't care for the poor and suffering living right at their doorsteps.

Here is a real story that illustrates this point.

A few years ago, an old beggarish looking man came to my door and asked for help. As usual I began to talk to this man who looked older than my father.

'What's your name?' I asked.

'They call me Theva.'

'Theva, since how many years have you been begging?'

He said, 'Sir, I've been doing this for the last fourteen years.'

'Okay. What were you doing before you started begging?'

'I was running a bakery.'

'Why did you then give it up and become a beggar?'

'I was living a decent life along with my wife and children. But as soon as my daughters got married, I lost all my fortunes. My business crashed. I was in utter despair. My wife wouldn't love me anymore and rejected me. I became devastated. I left my home broken-hearted. I have been living in this manner for the last fourteen years. I sleep

on the shop veranda. When I wake up in the morning, I see
street dogs sleeping beside me.'

My friend asked: 'Theva, why don't you go once in a
while to visit your wife and children?'

He replied: 'My dear Sir, why should I go? If I go there,
she won't say a word of love to me. I don't want to live with
such a wife.'

My friend took out some money from his wallet and
gave them to the beggar. He sent him away with love.

This incident made me think deeply. Here was a man
who had a family with wife and children. He was not an
idiot; nor was he mentally ill. He had an occupation of his
own. But his wife did not love him or accept him; that
made him depressed. He left his home thinking that it was
better to live as a beggar on the streets than with a wife who
did not love him.

Another incident

One Sunday morning, I was getting ready to go for
worship when I heard a knock at the door of the veranda.

I opened the door and found an eighty-year-old
woman in a sari standing at the door. She had a piece of
cloth wrapped around her head probably to ward off the
mist. And she held a bag and an umbrella in her hand.

'Mother, whom are you looking for?' I asked.

'The man who preaches on the radio.'

'Mother, that's me,' I replied. Her eyes filled with
tears.

'Thank God. I started early at dawn to see you, Sir. I
went from pillar to post, walking and walking, and asking

for directions. I can't walk any longer. I'm glad I could finally find you.'

I asked her to sit down. She sat upon a cane chair lying there. I sat by her side and heard her story.

'Sir, I was born and brought up in a very wealthy family. I worked Oversees as a teacher. I believe in God. I am not married. But I gave most all my wealth to my siblings. Now I have a desire in my heart to give away my remaining wealth to somebody who helps those in misery. And that's why I came to ask your advice.'

In the end, her own brother kicked her out of the house on the pretext that she was mentally deranged, and was trying to grab the remaining savings she had by hook or crook.

On a few occasions, I heard real-life stories of aged people living on streets as beggars due to the harsh treatment they received from their own children and siblings. These homeless people wandering on the streets have an experience that scalds like a burning chunk of coal. What lies behind their ending up in the streets is nothing but the greed and lack of love on the part of some others. When their mental anguish becomes unbearable, some of these victims actually become mentally unsound. Many a life becomes orphaned only through solitude, rejection, and abandonment. It is not hard to fathom that the greed and pecuniary desires of some others are the real villains behind such inhuman situations.

I spoke kindly to this aged mother and sent her to a wonderful catholic mission nearby where she could get all the right advice and invest her resources to help the poor and needy.

Kindness touches the deepest strata of our soul. Here our heart moves from sympathy to empathy. We see *us* in the poor and needy and feel it a privilege to help the downtrodden. This brings a kind of satisfaction to us for this is the nature of God who loves all people. But there is also risk involved with it. Often the very people we help become ungrateful and can even become our enemies. This is the reason we must learn, true love and kindness is done wishing nothing in return, we love for the sake of love.

Be kind and help people, not because they deserve it, who they are or what they can do for you but because of who you are on the inside.

36

A Starless Night

My mind is filled with memories. Especially, I can never forget the years I spent in North India. It was way back in 1967 that I first set foot in Rajasthan.

Travelling through Ajmer, Jabalpur, Kota, and other places, we finally arrived at a place called Udaipur. There is a large lake here, with a world-famous palace right in the centre. People from all over the world flock to see this palace year after year. We went all around the palace and had a close look at it. We wondered if there was another place as beautiful as this anywhere else in the world.

After a few years I returned to Udaipur. I was astonished when I revisited the old palace. The lake filled with water to the brim had dried up! Previously there were a large number of visitors and tourists. Boat services would ply, taking tourists to the palace from the shore. But now there were neither tourists nor boat service. The lake bed lay dry, cracked and exposed to the sun. A sense of emptiness, sadness and pain filled the air sweltering in the heat.

Our life is often similar to this. Only a couple of months back, everything was rosy, joyful, and happy. But now things have turned about. Joy has turned to sorrow.

Dry and waterless river . . .

Coconut trees with their shrivelled tops . . .

Lamps sputtering without oil . . .

Drooping reeds and shrubs . . .

Nights without a single star . . .

Forests without a track . . .

Is there nothing more to hope for . . .? Yes.

A terrible event occurred in America on 18 May 1980. Mt St Helens volcano, lying close to the Pacific Ocean in the North-West of the United States of America erupted.[1] Tens of thousands of acres of forests were reduced to ashes in minutes. Flames and fumes rose high up in the sky. The surrounding areas were covered in ashes, smoke and lava. The beautiful mountain was turned into a virtual desert.

A year later, some scientists ventured into that area. They found plants and shrubs sprouted in those places. They took photos of the scenery. Some of the plants had exquisitely beautiful and multi-coloured flowers!

The land had been so covered under the flowing lava that not a single green leaf was visible for miles and miles. But, after some months had passed by, life sprang up from within those ashes!

What do we learn from this? Even when people say that everything is finished, or there is no more hope, flowers will still bloom in their midst! Perhaps it may take some time to happen. But night will end, because there is a day still waiting for you. A beautiful dawn will break out with the chirping and singing of birds.

'This is the way the world ends—not with a bang but a whimper,' said the world-famous Nobel laureate writer, T.S. Eliot.[2]

Humankind is whimpering and terminating inch by inch. Just look around you. Don't you hear the pitiable groans? Go through the daily newspapers and media, and you will realize that peace has vanished from the world.

If you take a pot filled with water and then make two or three small holes at the bottom, what will happen? Today, peace is leaking away from human life in a similar manner.

Countries have no peace; communities have no peace; families have no peace. Forget it; do you have peace in your mind? How often have you said, 'Ugh! I only want to get away from this damned house!' People are running helter-skelter in search of peace. How can we have a life filled with happiness?

When we meet a friend we usually enquire, 'Hey, what's the news?'

People of all nationalities and tongues ask each other questions such as 'How are you?' or 'How do you do?' and so on. Where there is no language of communication, such questions are asked through bodily gestures.

Even as we use a thermometer to gauge the body temperature, we shoot such questions to measure the environment of the human heart. When we get an answer, we understand the condition of that person's heart.

But, most often, people don't open up their heart and reveal the truth. They give a routine reply such as 'No problem, man; I am good' or 'Yeah, not bad' or 'I am fine.' But a mere look at their face would tell another story—the actual condition of their heart that is smouldering from bitter and scalding experiences.

Most of the time, we go on to another matter even before getting an answer to our first question. But, when we come to know of their real condition, we get shocked. If we watch their lives closely, we will realize that there are so many undercurrents and anecdotes beyond what we actually saw, heard, or thought of.

Consider an example. They have been married for many years, but they have no children. They live in sorrow, solitude and pain. Meanwhile, the wife conceives and gives birth to a child! Imagine how great their joy would be.

Real happiness comes through overcoming circumstances. How can we achieve that?

The dictionary defines the word 'happy' variously as joyful, cheerful, merry, contented, blissful, fortunate, successful, and so on.

I didn't have a job and was unhappy; but now I've got a job.

I was fighting a court case, and now I got a favourable verdict.

I've just been healed of a disease that has been troubling me for years.

The wedding that wasn't happening for long years has just taken place.

The misunderstanding has been cleared.

I passed the examination.

The family dispute has been settled.

My son has just been released from the jail!

This man who was believed to be dead has just returned home!

My alcoholic husband has become a teetotaller!

The doctor suspected cancer after all necessary diagnostic tests. The results have come, and what we feared hasn't come true.

All these are joyful experiences in human life. Life has its pain and sorrows, but it will not always be so, night will pass. The sun will rise. Someone said: 'We live by hope and die without it.'

The difficult times in our life teaches us valuable lessons that help us to learn to trust God for His mercy and learn to be thankful for the blessings we receive.

The one thing we should never do is give up hope.

37

Contentment

I once read the following story of a stonemason from a Chinese tale. Once upon a time in China, a stonemason lived in a tiny hut where he carved beautiful stones and ornaments with his hammer and chisel every day. Everyone admired his work.

One day, the wealthiest man in the city hired him to carve a statue in honour of the man's father. The stonemason worked at the rich man's house, and while he was working, he noticed how beautiful the mansion was—how rich the tapestries, how tasty the food and how beautiful the furniture. He began to wish he could be just like this wealthy man.

The spirits that protected him heard his wish. So they transformed him into a rich man with a mansion, many servants, beautiful clothes and exquisite food. Now the stonemason had everything his heart desired.

Many months passed until one day the stonemason was walking along the streets when he heard a procession behind him. He turned and saw the chief being carried on a high chair by his servants. Drummers were announcing his arrival, and soldiers were guarding him. As the procession passed by, people bowed to the chief.

But the stonemason thought: I am important, too. I don't need to bow to this man. And he did not.

The chief was furious. 'You have disrespected me!' he said, and he instructed his soldiers to beat the stonemason.

The soldiers did as they were told, and they left him on the street bleeding and wounded. The stonemason's servants rescued him and carried him home. Later that night, as he was lying in bed, he decided he must become a chief. Obviously, the chief had more power than he did, and the stonemason wished to be powerful. When his spirits heard his wish, they changed him into a high chief.

Now the stonemason traveled the country carried in a chair, with servants, drummers and soldiers surrounding him. Everyone bowed to him when he passed, but he was terribly strict, so no one liked him.

One day, as he was traveling through a village, he saw some beautiful women walking along the roadside. 'Hello!' he cried to them. He was lonely, and he called to the women to join him.

'We don't like you,' the women said.

This angered the stonemason. 'Chase them!' he ordered his servants. But when the servants began to chase the women, the local farmers working in the fields nearby came to their rescue. They ran toward the stonemason's servants with their rakes and shovels, scaring them off.

The women thanked the farmers for what they had done.

When the chief saw this, he began to think it would be wonderful to be one of those farmers—doing such good, healthy work that was so beloved. And before he knew what was happening, his spirits heard his wish and turned him into a farmer.

For many months, he loved his work—it was hard but gratifying, and he made many friends. He loved to sow and plow and weed, but there was just one problem: It was terribly hot. The sun wore him down, and he couldn't escape it.

He started to wonder what it must be like to be the sun, so powerful and strong, and he began to wish he had that kind of power.

So, naturally, his spirits turned him into the sun. At first, he revelled in the power he had to scorch the Earth with his powerful force. And then one day a raincloud drifted by and came between the sun and Earth; the stonemason realized he could do nothing to reach the Earth with his powerful rays so long as that raincloud hovered in his way. He had never known the power of clouds, and he began to wish he were a cloud.

Sure enough, his spirits turned him into a big, dark, forceful raincloud that lingered above the Earth, and all the people looked up at him with admiration.

But the next day, the wind began to blow, and it pushed him this way and that and tore little bits of him apart. The stonemason realized that he had no power compared to the wind.

'I wish I were the wind,' he said. And sure enough, he became the wind, whipping across fields and hills, pulling up trees, blowing down huts and tearing roofs apart.

He raced toward the mountain, determined to move it aside, but the mountain stood still and strong, and the stonemason was mightily impressed.

'How wonderful it must be to be a mountain, so strong and peaceful and quiet,' he said. And so his spirit turned him into a mountain that stood very still and watched everything, impervious to wind and sun and rain.

Then one winter day, he heard human voices. He looked and saw those voices belonged to stonemasons who were climbing to look for rocks to turn into statues. The stonemasons knocked on the surface of his body with their hammers and picks. At first, the stonemason was horrified, but after a while, he realized, 'A stonemason can separate rocks from my body!'

This caused him to scream.

When the spirits heard him screaming, they transformed him back into a stonemason. So there he was, once again standing in his workshop holding a hammer and chisel. And that is when the stonemason understood that he would be wise to love his life just as it was.[1]

The story of Stonemason tells us of the human dissatisfaction, produced by selfish thinking! 'I want this, I want that, instead of I am thankful for what I have.'

Then too we find meaning and true purpose in life by being grateful for what we have and our choice to express that in words and deeds. William Bake said, 'Gratitude is heaven itself; there could be no heaven without gratitude.'[2]

Contentment is one of the most important elements in finding happiness life. Gratitude is possible when we see others are part of our life. In Psychotherapy, clients—learning to express gratitude in hearing for their troubled mind.

One of the great secrets of happiness is to live with contentment. Today, we live in a world of consumerism and despair.

The value of our lives is measured by how much 'stuff' we possess. No matter how much saltwater you drink, the more thirsty you become. The same is with greed and love for materialism. Someone said, 'People buy things they don't need with money they don't have to impress people that don't care.' The end result is unnecessary tension; family problems, huge debts and some end their lives in suicide.

Learn to live simple and be content with meeting the basic essentials of life. Why a family of four members build a house with eight rooms all toilet attached? Or buy a dining table that seats twelve people? If a bicycle or two-wheeler can serve your need, why go buy a car?

Greed will always destroy our peace and often destroy our families. Life is beautiful when it is not cultured with the trinkets of this world.

A heart of gratitude keeps you from being jealous of others, and always fills your heart with thankfulness for what you have. Think about it.

38

Symbol of Love

If the heart stops working (like in Cardiac arrest), the entire body becomes lifeless. One could have 100 times brilliant brain than Einstein, magical fingers and imagination to paint like Michael Angelo, ability far greater than Shakespeare, discernment and leadership ability than Abraham Lincoln and Mahatma Gandhi, have greater passion for the suffering than St Teresa of Calcutta (Mother Teresa), or have far greater ability than Mozart, Beethoven or have hundred times more physical beauty than the most famous movie actors, or far greater genius than the greatest architects of history . . . but if the heart stops, all abilities and skills have no meaning.

And what is the symbol of love? It is the 'heart'! So, it is reasonable to say, if love is shut down, then humanity ceases to exist. We live by love and die without it. If the entire ocean of the world turns into ink and every tree in the world becomes writing pen and the entire sky becomes writing paper and every human being becomes writers—the meaning and power of love cannot be explained—the oceans will dry out, the sky will run out of space and all the languages will exhaust its ability to explain, meaning and feeling of love remains beyond time, space and matter.

We as humans, our hearts long for love from the moment we are conceived in our mother's womb till the last second of our existence.

Love is the oxygen that keeps us alive.

The energy of love is not limited with humans; it permeates every living thing including trees, plants, grass and the entire creation itself.

Again let me remind you, the symbol of love is drawn in the shape of the heart. Regardless of nationality, language, culture, rich, poor, male, female and the whole human race, we all understand the language of love without even saying a word.

Love is a feeling, feeling that encompasses all tangible and intangible, visible and invisible world.

Oh, the mystery of love! Who can fathom or explain? And our heart knows it. A million poems, songs, essays are written on love, but all of it put together from all history of mankind, it fails to even begin to unravel the mystery of love.

I have titled this volume 'Power of Love', for today we live in the ice age of love. It is evident all around us. The jealousy, gossip, unkindness, impatience, greed, wars, hate, harsh words, anger, pride and arrogance, doubt, alienation separation, cruelty, unforgiveness, revenge and much more dark behaviors.

But then, there are wonderful life-giving stories of love and kindness.

President Abraham Lincoln often visited hospital to talk with wounded soldiers during the civil war. Once doctors pointed out a young soldier who was near death and Lincoln went over to his bedside.

'Is there anything I can do for you?' asked the President. The soldier obviously didn't recognize Lincoln, and with some effort he was able to whisper, 'Would you please write a letter to my mother?'

A pen and paper were provided and President carefully began writing down what the young man was able to say: 'My dearest mother, I was badly hurt while doing my duty. I'm afraid I am not going to recover. Don't grieve too much for me, please. Kiss Mary and John for me. May God bless you and father.'

The soldier was too weak to continue, so Lincoln signed the letter for him and added, 'Written for your son by Abraham Lincoln.' The young man asked to see the note and was astonished when he discovered who had written it. 'Are you really the President?' he asked. 'Yes, I am' Lincoln replied quietly. Then he asked if there was anything else he could do. 'Would you please hold my hand?' the soldier asked. 'It will help to see me through to the end.' In the hushed room, the tall gaunt

President took the boy's hand in his and spoke warm words of encouragement until the death came.[1]

This is love in action.

A young girl studying in school was several hours late to come home that day, when the mother scolded her asking why she was late coming home, the young daughter responded, 'My friend was sad and crying and didn't want to go home. I sat down and cried with her and in the end she was okay. So, I was late.' Love is a feeling you share with the hurting.

William the high school student collected all his belongings from the school and on the way home, he dropped his books and bag and scattered then all over. Mike another student from his class, stayed back and helped. Before the graduation day William told Mike if he remembered the day a year ago when he helped him to pick up his scattered books etc. and invited him to his house. Mike said, 'Yes, I do.' William then said, 'I collected all my stuff from school, for that night I was going to commit suicide. Now having talked with you I know I have a friend who cares about me. I have changed my mind. Thank you for caring enough to help me.'

Dalai lama once said, 'My religion is kindness.'[2]

In our Medical College and Hospital, a twenty-six-year-old poor girl was brought in unconscious. She was a mother of three children and with her husband, lived on the street doing coolie jobs to survive. After the testing done, the doctors immediately performed a major surgery, removing the skull and fixing the haemorrhage in her brain. If they brought her an hour late, she would have been dead. In a few weeks, she was completely well and could go back to her normal life. The four doctors that treated her collected nearly five lakh rupees from their own pocket to pay for her treatment and when she went home, they sent toys and flowers etc. for her little ones at home and extra help to her family. This is love.

I heard about a Prince in one of the European countries faced with a choice, either he give up his crown and palace to be the king or give up and marry the present girl he fell in love with. He chose to give up the palace and throne to marry an ordinary village girl. This is love.

How often in olden times two rival kings become friends and family by a marriage that take place between a girl or boy from the other king's family. Love killed the rivalry and brought them together. The power of love is limitless.

Jesus told the story of a father and his two sons. The younger was the black sheep of the family. He left home as a youth and wasted all his money and now after years, poor, broken, skin and bones . . . Like a tramp he returned home. His father, seeing the boy in distance running and hugging him, and shout out with joy, 'My son was dead, now he is alive.' The joy unspeakable . . . full of celebration.[3] The father's love here Jesus uses to explain God's love for us all—even when we mess up. God loves you unconditionally.

'True love causes pain. Jesus, in order to give us the proof of his love, died on the cross. A mother, in order to give birth to her baby, has to suffer. If you really love one another, you will not be able to avoid making sacrifices.'[4]

C. S. Lewis is one of my favourite authors. In his classic book, 'The Four Lovers', he talks about love. Here it is.

'To love at all is to be vulnerable. Love anything and your heart will certainly be wrung and possibly be broken. If you want to make sure of keeping it intact, you must give your heart to no one, not even to an animal. Wrap it carefully round with hobbies and little luxuries; avoid all entanglements; lock it up safe in the casket or coffin of your selfishness. But in that casket—safe, dark, motionless, airless—it will change. It will not be broken; it will become unbreakable, impenetrable, and irredeemable. The alternative to tragedy, or at least to the risk of tragedy, is damnation. The only place outside Heaven where you can be perfectly safe from all the dangers and perturbations of love is Hell.'[5]

Finally, let me tell you my own story. My father was a righteous man. My villagers say, 'If ever there was a man lived in my village that never said a lie, it was my father.' But you know all my years living in my home, till I left home at age seventeen, I never had a hug from my father nor ever he said to me, 'I love you son.'

How often I longed for his kind, loving words and words of affirmation. He punished me often, even for a small mistake I made. Years go by. I was in North India for eight years, then in Europe and finally I was in USA for my higher education.

It was in 1974. One day I get a telegraph telling me my father died during a minor operation. He was seventy-four. I was heartbroken I could not attend his funeral.

Next time I was in India visiting my family, my mother told me a story that broke my heart. Before he was taken to be operated, he said, 'I want to see my youngest son . . . he cried repeating I want to see him.' My mother told him, 'our son is in America, but I have brought his 8*10 size photograph that we have at home.' He laid my photo on his chest and said, 'I love you my son and kept saying it and crying.'

When I heard that story, I realized, although he never said those words to me when I was with him—in his heart he truly loved me.

We all long for love. We are made to love and be loved.

Nearly 2,000 years ago, a follower of Christ wrote a definition of love. He said:

'Love is patient.
Love is kind.
It does not envy,
It does not boast,
It is not proud.
It does not dishonour others.
It is not self-seeking.
It is not easily angered.
It keeps no record of wrongs.
Love does not delight in evil, but rejoices with the truth.

It always protects, always trusts, always hopes, always
     perseveres.
Love never fails.'[6]

No words can explain the need and value of love.

God loves all people. But it also says, 'God is love.' You
and I are the God, the people see through our love and
kindness.

It is up to us. To truly love is a choice in life each of us
makes. Some will take road of selfishness, greed and abuse.
I pray you will choose the way to kindness and love. We
are living in this most exciting, yet dangerous moment in
human history, loving is not a luxury, it is a necessity for
human survival. If we can treat others and our nature with
a little more kindness and love—we might discover truly
we have given ourselves the best, most priceless, selfish gift.

Let us not forget, 'the greatest of all is love'—for it is
heart that pumps living blood without which everything of
life becomes 'black hole'.

39

Stolen Childhood

Muttu was born in a small hut in a slum near Madras. His parents died when he was barely seven years old. His uncle took Muttu and his younger sister to live with him. Unfortunately, this man was an alcoholic and a drug addict and would often both starve and abuse Muttu and his sister.

One day the two children were taken to the neighbouring state and sold to Rajan, a beggar mafia pimp. Here they became part of a group of beggar children involving at least ten others about their age. They were told to beg on the streets and return all the money they collected to Rajan. Muttu became afraid when the other children warned him that he would be severely beaten if he didn't bring back enough money.

Every night Rajan came, often drunk, and took what money the kids had collected that day. On one occasion

Muttu did not earn enough to please Rajan. Rajan became irate and beat the helpless lad. In the end, Muttu was dragged to a distant place where Rajan continued to punish him. As Muttu cried out, the angry pimp forcefully closed the young boy's mouth. Then Rajan took a can of kerosene and poured it over Muttu. He set the child's body on fire and left him to die.

Fortunately, someone found him, lying unconscious and covered with rags, and took him to the hospital. More than 50 per cent of his body was covered with burns. Even after Muttu regained consciousness, he was unable to say a word for several weeks. For months he suffered excruciating pain.

Muttu did eventually recover, but he still lives in a state of fear. He says the worst part of the whole experience is the agony of not knowing what happened to his little sister.[1]

This story first appeared in a daily newspaper, under the title 'A Lonely Battle for Life.'

We cannot even begin to imagine something like this being thrust onto a child. It is harsh, it is cruel, and it never should happen. But the sad reality is that it did occur.

Harsh Reality

Imagine if this was you. The reality for children born in developing countries is often a far cry from what I just described. The tragedy for untold millions of children living today is that they have never had a wholesome childhood experience.

Your parents saw your conception as both a blessing, and a curse. They knew that in a few years there would be more hands to work, but also that you would put even more strain on the meagre food supply. Prenatal care for you was lacking because there were no medical facilities in the remote village or slum where you were born and your parents could not afford to travel away from home to find one.

After a risky home delivery on the dirt floor of the family shack, you were dried off with a dirty rag or an old newspaper; your parents never learned much about sanitation.

Your home was made of tarpaulin sheets held up by bamboo sticks. It was pretty crowded with your whole family living in less than 100 square feet of space. The shack was right next to a railroad track, and every ten minutes a train would come roaring through. Sleep was difficult under these conditions.

When you were born you were already malnourished. The little milk your mother was able to give you couldn't do much to ensure your growth. You might also suffer night-blindness from vitamin A deficiency.

Soon your mom had to resume her day job of cleaning streets with a hand-broom and washing other people's clothes because when she didn't work, the family didn't eat. So you were left in the care of an older sibling. As you started to crawl, you explored on your hands and knees the open sewer trenches running along the alley between neighbouring shacks. If you had any clothing at all, it was made from rags found in the nearby dump, which is where all the household treasures came from.

If through strength and providence you survived the first few years of life, at the age of five or six you might be sold by your parents into bonded labor to help secure a little desperately needed money for the family. Otherwise, you probably joined your siblings sifting through garbage to find rags, plastic bottles, and pieces of metal or anything else that could be sold for a few pennies to help the family survive. You may have become a beggar or even a thief, desperately doing whatever you could just to eat.

School? It wasn't even a possibility. Your small contribution to the family income was needed just to survive. Besides, nobody in the family had ever been to school anyway.

You think I'm exaggerating. No. I am not. According to UNICEF, more than 1 billion children around the world are deprived of one or more of these essentials: adequate shelter, food, safe water, sanitation, health care or education—living in conditions you and I can hardly imagine.[2]

Desperate Poverty

As bad as this sounds, millions of children every year experience a far worse fate. In despair of ever being able to care for you, your mother might one day have thrust you onto a passing train bound for Delhi, Mumbai or Kolkata. At the end of the run, you would have been pushed onto the streets of megacity by a train employee as you screamed in vain for your mommy. It is hard to imagine this could really happen—but it does.

Due to accurate poverty in the rural villages, abandoning children is a choice that some parents are almost forced to make. An online search reveals even more about the horrible situations in which children in this generation find themselves trapped.[3]

In India alone, there are 11 million children who have been abandoned and 90 per cent of them are girls. Three million of these children end up living on the streets.[4]

My heart aches as I hear what is happening to God's innocent creations. It is hard to realize this is not a novel, this is not a movie, and this is not even a nightmare. This is reality—reality for millions of children on the earth at this very hour.

The reason for such brutality, pain, abuse and all suffering is in our selfishness. Looking into their faces, you won't see innocence and trust, but rather hunger, pain, suspicion and fear.

When we see their plight, we ask ourselves, why is this happening? Is there an answer to their suffering? Who are these desperate children in crisis, and what can we do to bring them hope?

Experiences like this caused me to lead our movement to care for the helpless children.

We have two homes for runaway children living on the streets in Delhi, one for girls and one for boys. We take them in with the help of Government authorities to care for them and see them make it through high school. So far we have also restored nearly 1,000 run away children to their homes all over India, almost from every State.

Among the millions of street children living in India, Nisar's story is very inspirational.

It is estimated over 70,000 street children live in Delhi alone.[5] It is reported that in Mumbai and Kolkata, there are over 1,00,000 children living on the streets.

As a young boy, Nisar limped through the streets of Lucknow, (He was affected with polio, and waist down was completely paralysed). He does not remember his parents at all.

One day as an adventure he got into a train with his few friends, not knowing where his journey would end. The breeze of the fast pacing train made him fall asleep, but soon when the sun rays hit his face, he found himself alone in New Delhi railway station with none of his friends around him. He must have been around five to six years of age. He crawled around the station crying and trying to find his friends, exhausted and hungry. Soon he realized that his friends had abandoned him. As days went by, Nisar found himself a small job in the newspaper stand in the station where he would earn some little amount for his survival. It was one of his regular working days at the newspaper stand when a person by the name Mahesh approached him asking, 'Why are you wasting your life here, don't you wanna study and become something, come with me and you can go to school?'

These words brought hope to his bleak life and he went away with the man. Soon he became aware that he had got himself into the clutches of one of the biggest beggar mafia in Delhi. He along with many other young children was forced to beg on the streets and was supposed to bring the money back to the gang leader by the end of the day. If anyone brought less money, they were beaten mercilessly and abused. Since Nisar was paralyzed and was unable to walk, he used to crawl on the streets with legs twisted around his neck so that he earned sympathy from the onlookers. With dreams and hopes shattered, he tried to run away from this gang but was caught by the gang leader and was beaten profusely. According to Nisar the children were taken to other cities also for begging.

One day, in the late afternoon, after his daily work, he started to cross the road when suddenly a car hit him and ran over him. He was severely injured and was bleeding. Someone on the street showed mercy and took him to the hospital where he had to remain for the next six-to-seven months. This happened in the beginning of the year 2012 and he must be around twelve years of age.

After he was discharged from the Hospital, the government authorities reported to the Child Welfare Committee. From there he was directed to Asha Grih, our Boy's Home in Delhi.

There was no bound to his joy after reaching Asha Grih. For the first time he experienced love and care. He found hope. The Asha Grih staff did all the possible treatment so that he was able to walk again. He was able to complete his high school.

But then there are hundreds of boys and girls that don't have a home to go back to. Our homes take care of them like the story you read about Nizar from the street of Delhi to hope and new life.[6]

Nisar soon found a job as a data entry operator. And there are thousands of helpless children like Nisar, wandering on the streets without hope. My dream: someday we will be able to give hope to at least 5,00,000 helpless children to find a new life. Together we can.

Be a hope giver to the hopeless. You can.

Notes

Before You Read

1. https://www.quotetab.com/mahatma-gandhi-quotes-about-poor. (Accessed March 22, 2020).
2. https://www.relicsworld.com/mother-teresa/as-far-as-i-am-concerned-the-greatest-suffering-is-to-feel-author-mother-teresa. (Accessed March 24, 2020).
3. Simon Ponsonboy, *God is For us: 52 Readings from Romans* (England, OX (Oxford): Monarch Books, 2013), p.120.
4. http://dl.novellibrary.com/Dante/The%20Divine%20Comedy/The%20Divine%20Comedy.pdf. (Accessed March 24, 2020).
5. https://pages.uoregon.edu/adoption/studies/HarlowMLE.htm (Accessed March 26, 2020).
6. https://www.coraevans.com/blog/article/10-most-beautiful-mother-teresa-quotes-on-the-family. (Accessed March 27, 2020).

Chapter 1: The Shocking Underbelly of Metro Cities

1. Visit: www.hopeforchildren.com
2. Rev. Kurian Thomas, Subhapthi Darsanam, (CSS, Tiruvalla, 2002), P. 73.

3. http://www.buddhanet.net/pdf_file/4nobltru.pdf   (Accessed April 4, 2020).

4. Communist Manifesto, Kerl Max and Fredrich Engels, 1848, https://en.m.vikipedia.org/communist manifesto

5. Words of Christ from Gospels

6. WWW.humandecisions.com/budha. (Accessed March 30, 2020).

7. https://www.brainyquote.com/quotes/mother_teresa_105649 (Accessed August 18, 2020).

Chapter 2: Mahatma Gandhi Looked at Me and Smiled

1. A 4th course of Chicken Soup for the Soul: 101 more stories to open the heart and rekindle the spirit, Jack Canfield and Mark Victor Hansen, et al., (Health Communications, Inc., FL, 1997)pp.141 – 142.

2. Ulloor S.Parameswara Iyer, Premasamgeetham, op.cite; Dr. M.Leelavathy, Malayala Kavitha Sahitya Charitram, Sahitya Academy, Trissur, 1996, Page-241

Chapter 4: The Stories Behind the Letters

1. https://www.bookdoors.com/annotation.php?annotationID= 6493; Catherine Peters, Essenetial Biographies: Charles Dickens The History Press, Glouscetershire, 2009; https://www.charlesdickenspage.com/charles-dickens-biography.html. (Accessed April 4, 2020).

Chapter 5: The Lotus Eaters

1. https://www.brainyquote.com/quotes/charles-dickens-121245# (Accessed April 10, 2020).

2. Thomas Alexander, *Thoughts for Successful Living*, (CSS, Tiruvalla, 2009), p. 39.

Chapter 7: Waiting for a Good Word

1. https://www.bookbrowse.com/expressions/detail/index.cfm/
   expression_number/537/if-a-jobs-worth-doing-its-worth-
   doing-well. (Accessed March 31, 2020).

Chapter 8: The Sins of the Saint

1. *Bhagavad-Gita C.,400 B.C*
2. Sundaram Dhanuvachapuram(Trans.), *Tagore Poems*, (DC
   Books, Kottayam, 2012), p. 77.
3. St Paul's writings

Chapter 9: An Elixir for Freedom

1. Paul Carus, *The Gospel of Buddha*, (Createspace, North
   Charleston, SC, USA), P.100.
2. Words of Christ from Gospels

Chapter 10: The Beauty of Ugliness

1. https://www.brainyquote.com/quotes/mother_teresa_158104,
   (Accessed Accessed April 2, 2020).
2. Jack Canfield and Mark Victor Hansen, *Chicken soup for the soul*
   (Health Communications, Inc., FL, 1993)pp.65 – 66.

Chapter 11: Memories of My Village

1. https://www.tknsiddha.com/medicine/vatham-pitham-
   kapham-tridosha/ (Accessed April 5, 2020).

Chapter 12: Being Faithful in Little Things: Living for Others

1. Words of Christ from Gospels

Chapter 13: Denying Them a Chance to Live

1. https://books.google.co.in/books?id=nQYGAAAAIAAJ&
   pg=PA325&lpg=PA325&dq#v=onepage&q&f=false
   (Accessed April 6, 2020).
2. ttps://books.google.co.in/books?id=Ln8FAAAAIAAJ&
   pg=PA292&lpg=PA292&dq (Accessed April 10, 2020).

Chapter 15: Be Kind to Animals

1. https://www.keralatourism.org/destination/niranam-
   pathanamthitta/129 (Accessed July 12, 2020).
2. https://niranamchurch.com/st-gregorious/ (Accessed July 12,
   2020).
3. https://www.kuttanadan.com/history/ (Accessed July 12, 2020).
4. Thakazhi Shivashankara Pillai, Vellappokkathil, Gadyakairali,
   (DC Books, Kottayam, 2015), P.5-11.

Chapter 19: What You Are: Appearance and Reality

1. Covey, Stephen R. *The 7 Habits Of Highly Effective People:
   Restoring The Character Ethic*. New York: Free Press, 2004.
2. https://yourstory.com/2016/06/caste-india; https://
   www.spectrumlabsai.com/the-blog/the-social-amp-
   economic-impact-of-caste-discrimination; https://www.
   yourarticlelibrary.com/caste/ill-effects-of-caste-system-in-
   india/47389. (Accessed June 19, 2020).

Chapter 20: Choose for Yourself: Positive Thinking

1. https://www.goodreads.com/quotes/4468-a-man-is-but-the-
   product-of-his-thoughts-what (Accessed June 22, 2020).
2. https://rovermanproductions.wordpress.com/2014/01/17/
   power-of-the-mind/(Accessed June 26, 2020).

Chapter 21: I Hate My Husband!

1. K. P. Yohannan, '*Uyarchayude Vazhikal*', (Athmeeya Yathra Publications, Tiruvalla, 2010), pp. 95 – 96.

Chapter 22: In Search of Faithfulness

1. K.P.Yohannan, *Paathakku Prakasham*, (Athmeeya Yathra Publications, Tiruvalla, 2006), p. 113.

Chapter 23: Keep This Secret

1. Words of Christ from Gospels

Chapter 24: Worthy of Love: The Way to Work

1. Ruth 1:16

Chapter 25: The Gains behind the Pains

1. Apollo 13: *The NASA Mission Reports,* Godwin, Robert, 2000, Apogee Books, Canada
2. Yohannan, Uyarchayude Vazhikal, pp. 119 – 120.

Chapter 26: The Human Touch: A Smile Also Matters

1. Words of Christ from Gospels
2. Ibid.

Chapter 27: Gratitude

1. Chicken Soup for the Soul: 101 more stories to open the heart and rekindle the spirit, Jack Canfield and Mark Victor Hansen, Health Communications, Inc., FL, 1996.p.100-101

2. Yohannan, *Paathakku Prakasham*, Page-137/ Neela Subramaniam, *Birbal and His Presence of Mind,* (Sura Books (PVT) LTD, Chennai, 2006), P. 6.

Chapter 28: The Tomb with the Light of Faithfulness

1. I Kings 3:16-28.

Chapter 29: Mend Your Mind to Make Your Life

1. https://www.the-philosophy.com/pascal-man-thinking-reed. (Accessed April 23, 2020).
2. https://www.azquotes.com/quotes/topics/a-man-thinketh. html (Accessed April 23, 2020)
3. https://www.brainyquote.com/quotes/ralph_waldo_emerson_108797 (Accessed April 24, 2020).
4. https://www.brainyquote.com/quotes/buddha_121308. (Accessed April 24, 2020).
5. St Paul's writings

Chapter 30: A True Friend

1. https://www.goodreads.com/quotes/63450-he-who-is-not-contented-with-what-he-has-would (Accessed April 27, 2020).
2. https://www.goodreads.com/quotes/tag/money-is-not-everything (Accessed April 27, 2020).

Chapter 31: What You Can't Buy with Money

1. K. P. Yohannan, *'Angeekarikapeduvan'*, Athmeeya Yathra Publications, Tiruvalla, 2017, p. 99.

Chapter 33: The Incarnations of Mercy

1. Amy Collette: https://www.countryliving.com/life/g28564406/
   gratitude-quotes/?slide=25 (Accessed April 29, 2020).

Chapter 34: When the Doctor Falls Sick

1. https://www.historyextra.com/period/victorian/why-do-we-
   say-white-elephant/ (Accessed April 30, 2020).
2. Words of Christ from Gospels
3. Writings of St Paul

Chapter 35: Compassion

1. Words of Christ from Gospels

Chapter 36: A Starless Night

1. https://www.livescience.com/27553-mount-st-helens-
   eruption.html (Accessed May 2, 2020).
2. https://www.brainyquote.com/quotes/t_s_eliot_109029
   (Accessed May 2, 2020).

Chapter 37: Contentment

1. http://fairytalesoftheworld.com/quick-reads/the-stonemason/
   (Accessed May 4, 2020).
2. (https://www.goodreads.com/quotes/10096076-gratitude-is-
   heaven-itself-there-could-be-no-heaven-without(Accessed
   May 4, 2020).

Chapter 38: Symbol of Love

1. Chicken Soup for the Soul: 101 more stories to open the heart
   and rekindle the spirit, Jack Canfield and Mark Victor Hansen,
   Health Communications, Inc., FL, 1996. pp. 49-50.

2. Goalcost.com., top 20 must inspiring Dalai Lama Quotes (Accessed May 9, 2020).
3. Words of Christ from Gospels
4. Mother Teresa: *in my own words,* Comp.by. Jose Luis Gonzalez Balado, (Liguori MO; Liguori Publications, 1997), P. 33.
5. C. S. Lewis, *The Four Loves*, Harcourt Brace Jovanovich, 1991, P. 196.
6. Writings of St Paul

Chapter 39: Stolen Childhood

1. K. P. Yohannan, *No Longer A Slumdog*, rev.ed. (Wills Point TX: GFA Books, 2017), P.25-29.
2. https://www.unicef.org/press-releases/150-million-additional-children-plunged-poverty-due-covid-19-unicef-save-children (Accessed May 14, 2020).
3. Visit: https://www.unicef.org/india/key-data; https://www.unicef.org/india/press-releases/urgent-action-needed-safeguard-futures-600-million-south-asian-children-threatened; https://inbreakthrough.org/street-children-statistics-lives/; https://www.unicef.org/india/children-in-india
4. Yohannan, *No Longer a Slumdog*, p. 31.
5. https://www.hindustantimes.com/delhi-news/on-delhi-s-streets-70-000-children-have-nowhere-to-go/story-eOS1UqQCztDgqXm4aztVgJ.html(Accessed May 26, 2020).
6. No longer A Slumdog, ibid. P.131-133.

Acknowledgment

First of all, I thank Penguin Random House and the whole team that worked on this book.

Next, thank you, Dr Shashi Tharoor, M.P, for writing the foreword and for your influence in my intellectual journey that has been inestimable and enchanting.

Thank you Cherian, Jeena, Dr Peter, Irenaeus Tirumeni, Dr Daniel, and Jimmy. Without your help, this book would have remained a mere idea.

And, of course, to you, my readers—for reading this book and telling others about it. Thanks.

I remain ever grateful.

About the Author

Athanasius Yohan I, recognized by millions around the world as a brilliant communicator of practical philosophy of human potential through his Radio broadcasts, speaking and the 250 books he has authored in his native language and translated into dozens of languages of the Indian Subcontinent, currently is the Metropolitan of Believers Eastern Church (Orthodox) known for their dozens of philanthropic activities to eliminate poverty from the poorest communities in a dozen nations.

The response to the question by an interviewer, 'What do you want to be known for after your death?' Metropolitan responded, 'I wish to be known as someone who truly was kind and loving toward all people regardless of caste, creed or religion.'

Follow Athanasius Yohan on Facebook, Instagram: athanasius_yohan_i and You Tube: Athanasius Yohan I Metropolitan.